TO WARREN

LIGHT OF DARKNESS

LIGHT OF DARKNESS

(Based on Inspired Events)

EBENEZER O. MAKINDE

MADE FOR SUCCESS

Made for Success Publishing
P.O. Box 1775 Issaquah, WA 98027
www.MadeForSuccessPublishing.com

Distributed by Made for Success Publishing

First Printing
Library of Congress Cataloging-in-Publication data
Maiknde, Ebenezer O.
LIGHT OF DARKNESS (Based on Inspired Events)
p. cm.

LCCN: 2021946307

ISBN: 978-1-64146-680-6 (***hardback***)
ISBN: 978-1-64146-681-3 (***eBook***)
ISBN: 978-1-64146-682-0 (***Audiobook***)

Printed in the United States of America

For further information contact Made for Success Publishing
+14255266480 or email service@madeforsuccess.net

Chapter 1

The Heavenlies

—

December 9, 2019

Beautiful clouds graced the sky with streams of inconceivable color. Wonderful shafts of light shone just above their magnificent brilliance off into the distance, much grander than any fireworks that could ever be found on Earth. A delightful, magical rain had just ceased some hours before, but still, the temperature was perfect. Even when it rained or snowed, the weather remained ideal, beyond splendid wherever any heavenly being went. In this place, there was continuous daylight, a ceaseless stream of dazzling luster. Waves of beautiful colors punctuated the sky. The fragrance of the Commander,

His wonderful and delightful scent, was like a burst of alluring aroma in the air. The flowers that lined the ground were astoundingly vibrant and even turned and faced the direction where any being went. In this place, the Heavenlies, there were no shadows, no gloom, not an ounce of any darkness.

"Next. Next!" Hadrenial, the seraph, shouted as he folded his arms and stood with his back to the sturdy, lustrous gate. "Every time..." he shook his head. "They never cease to amaze me. Why do ***I*** always get stuck being the gatekeeper?" he muttered under his breath. "Why can't someone ***ELSE*** take this position for once?" Hadrenial was now looking in the direction of Ophaniel, who just happened to be passing by.

"Are you talking to ***me***?" Ophaniel said as he continued onward briskly. Ophaniel was fleet-footed, and each step appeared almost invisible as he walked. "You know you're the man for the job. No one else could do it better! Don't let the Boss see you moping." His voice tapered off as he turned a corner behind the pearly gate, presumably to retake his place closer to the throne.

This was the Heavenlies, the Commander King's country, and today was no ordinary day. The Chief of the Heavenlies, Hadrenial's Commander and Boss, had made a call for all the angels, the seraphim and the cherubim, in both the Heavenlies and on Earth, to present themselves before Him. They were each to come prepared with a thorough account of all their responsibilities in the realms in which they traversed.

Typically, only seven of the greatest, most powerful seraphim stood directly in the Commander's presence. First was Michael, who was one so prone to fighting, waging war, and seeking to resolve injustice that such meetings quite frankly annoyed him; Raphael, who usually enjoyed the short break from causing a stir in the waters of the Earth to attend to such business as it afforded him the needed time to dry off; Gabriel, who typically tagged alongside Michael but on occasion went off on his own ambitious military excursions; Uriel, whose aura was so bright and vibrant that it so often bothered many of the other angels; and Saraqael, who was known to be incredibly friendly, being the angel who ushered Earth Dwellers into the afterlife, putting on a kind and happy visage to show them there was absolutely nothing to fear.

In addition to those five, there was also Raguel, known as "Mr. Justice," an angel who frequently teared up merely seeing all of the other spirit beings gathered together in perfect harmony, all banding together in perfect unison; and Remiel, whose voice was so commanding it caused the Earth to shudder when he opened and spoke a single word from his lips. They were all unique and mighty angelic instruments in their own respective rights. But on special occasions, like today, the Commander would make the throne open, and a call would be put out to all the Heavenlies' angelic forces—including those who found the majority of their responsibilities moving throughout the face of the Earth. Typically, the long-stretched ladder from the Heavenlies to Earth where many of the angels ascended and descended saw little traffic, but on this day, it was as bustling and vibrant as ever. Just beyond the ladder, the seraphim formed the line leading to the pearly gate that would allow them into the Heavenlies and into the Chief Commander's presence.

"Next!" Hadrenial demanded again, his voice now raised another octave. "Hellooo!?" he called out to a group of clustering angels some 50 feet away. For some strange reason, they were congregating tightly together, and each of their heads was bowed as if to be inspecting something closely.

The "special occasion," as they called it, was a tedious, drawn-out process, and it required many hands and a full effort from all of the heavenly hosts. Thousands upon thousands took part in making the occasion possible. Hadrenial, in addition to being the lucky angel assigned to let each of the seraphim inside the heavenly gates upon checking them in, was also tasked with a more important job—keeping any unwanted, trespassing visitors out.

"Helloooo? What's the holdup? I said NEXT," he called out, shaking his head and tapping his foot anxiously. For some strange reason, the group continued to mingle, baffling the impatient seraph and testing the true length of his patience.

"Netzach." Hadrenial turned to the tiny seraph on his left, who had just returned from break and who had been assigned as his assistant.

"Yes, Hadra?" Netzach replied, still working on a bite of food.

"'Hadrenial,' please. Please go and find out what is holding those guys up, the ones congregating over there." Hadrenial pointed in their direction. "We've got to keep things moving, or our Commander will not be happy."

Netzach shook his head as he wiped some crumbs from his tiny little hands. "I will do my best. If you ask me, the guys are probably just chitchatting away again; likely lost in discussion about their excursions on Earth. Give me a few minutes; I'll get things moving." Netzach dashed away to investigate what exactly was keeping the other angels from approaching the gate. Even his job as an assistant was important, as he could find himself dealing with many different types of spirits who would frequently try to worm their way into the Heavenlies illegally.

Hadrenial took a deep breath, folded his arms, and waited, leaning back against the pearly gates. As he sat there, he pondered how much he longed for the entire day to be over—deep down, he simply wanted to retake his place singing praises to the throne. As he stood there and time passed, his head began to droop—he was beginning to fall asleep.

"Good riddance," he muttered as he pulled away from the gate and checked the time. Becoming more impatient, he begrudgingly decided to leave his post to meet the group of angels himself and scold them for holding up the line. He dropped his clipboard and his pen and moved at once in the direction of the lollygaggers. As he approached, however, he noticed something strange. The seraphim were circling something, someone—a familiar face. In between them stood another, like them in form but not in character, whom they saw as encroaching on their territory.

"This little scoundrel is responsible. I was wondering what was holding up my line," Hadrenial said.

Netzach stood there with the others, somewhat on the outskirts of the circle. He was shorter and stood on his toes so he could successfully peek inside.

Netzach, seeing his boss had now made his way over, turned his attention away from the circle and toward him. "Sorry, boss," Netzach said. "Looks like this is a step beyond my pay grade."

"Zachariel," Hadrenial quipped, shifting his attention, "what is this ***swindler*** doing here in the Heavenlies?"

Zachariel stood amid the angels, his arms folded across his chest, his face baring an intimidating scowl. "It looks like he's looking to get some face time with the Chief. Says he's here to get ***permission***," he emphasized, not removing his eyes from the trespasser.

"Again? When is he ***not*** looking to get permission from the Boss?" Hadrenial turned his attention to Lucifer, who was standing in between the host of angels, arms folded as if he were ready to take each of them on at once. "Lucifer, don't you know that our Commander has other, more important things to deal with than to speak with you?"

Lucifer smiled. "I'm here to present myself just as the others are. There's nothing wrong with that, is there?" he replied.

"Right. What is it you want this time?" Hadrenial responded. "Make it quick; you're holding up my line, you reprobate."

"Still clever with the words, I see. Looks like your comrades on Earth are becoming of less use these days. Those Earth Dwellers have found my men and me a bit more, shall I dare say, appealing. Tell me, how does it feel for your group to be growing less and less effective each and every day? Hmm? You're still all about the Chief here, huh?" Lucifer turned to do a quick 360, flipping his hands into the air before settling back into his position and locking eyes with the surrounding angels. "I'm glad I left this—this shell of a life. How can just ***one*** Being take all the praise for Himself? But that's okay; there's much more glory and power for me on Earth. Now, gentlemen, if you'll excuse me, I have an appointment with my Adversary."

Lucifer began to walk, or stroll, rather, and the throng of angels surrounding him slowly parted to each side, letting him pass. His pointy tail wagged back and forth like a tiny little stick with every step he took. Although he was no longer one of them, they knew their Commander had given him full access to the throne, even though he had long ago fallen from the Heavenlies, some say as fast as lightning. He now made his home in the air, throughout all the skies of Earth.

"Come, come now, Hadré," he simmered.

"Hadrenial. Hadrenial. Ha-dre-ni-al. It's Hadrenial."

"Whatever. It's time for you to take me past those big gates and directly to the inner courts of my Adversary. Daylight is wasting, and I have many devious things to do with those Earth Dwellers that I must get permission for and begin doing now."

Begrudgingly, Hadrenial followed along, knowing that there was nothing he or the other angels could do to stop the devil's request from being seen.

***

The devil's movements were slippery and sly—he maneuvered like a serpent before the throne. His stubby little tail still whipped back and forth behind him while his chin remained held high arrogantly.

"So, you see, Your Highness, I've been doing a great deal of thinking lately, and I have a proposition that I know You will not refuse," Lucifer said, strolling back and forth as he scratched his chin with one hand and held the other behind his back. The words came from his lips with a great deal of calculation and cunning, as if to be delicately withering like a hunter through high grass, trying his best not to alarm his prey.

"Where have you come from, and what is it you want, Lucifer? It seems as if your requests are becoming more and more frequent," the Chief responded.

"I've been in Your presence but three times," Lucifer shot back with an innocent shrug.

"Three times... in the past week," Gabriel, who was also near the throne, fired back, challenging Lucifer's assertion. Gabriel was known as one never to back down from a challenge, which was why he and Michael had become close comrades. At that moment, his arms began to tighten, and his fists clenched with a sudden flash of rage. It caught the devil by surprise, and he stopped for a moment in his tracks. He slumped his shoulders in a defeated manner and lowered his head, fixing his eyes upon the ground.

"Yes, yes. Three times," he responded, regaining his composure. He strolled a few more times and then stopped, pivoting and protruding his chest to Gabriel and speaking directly to him.

"Is that ***a problem***?" he answered back. Without waiting for an answer, he began to saunter again.

"Lucifer." The Chief's voice was a resounding thunder. Whenever He spoke, those in His presence straightened their backs, becoming all the more silent.

Lucifer stopped and, at once, came to attention. "Yes, Your Highness," he answered.

"You still have not answered Me," the Commander said.

"I'm sorry, Your Highness, it seems that I must have forgotten the question," Lucifer replied sheepishly.

"Where have you come from?" the Commander asked.

The devil began to quietly mutter under his breath, his forehead nearly parallel to the ground. "Mr. Omnipotence Himself is curious as to what a poor little devil like me is doing? Could it be? I'm honored that I've become the apple of Your eye, Your Highness..."

"Answer the question, Lucifer," the Chief commanded.

"Of course! Yes. Your question. My men and I have been patrolling the Earth, of course, going back and forth and back and forth within it. Have You dropped in on Your chosen country lately? Or, shall I dare say, once chosen. There's already so much evil to see; it's quite wonderful."

"As I knew you would be," the Commander responded. "Have you found any prospects?"

"Today I come with no prospects, only plans."

"Oh really? What type of plans? Please amuse Me."

"Only the most devious, as You know, Your Highness."

"Make them plain, Lucifer."

"At your request. As you know, it's nearing the beginning of the new decade, and I would like to release something wonderful throughout all the Earth that will destroy, I mean test, Your people and all the other Earth Dwellers."

"Lucifer, you of all agents should know that I do not dwell nor operate in time."

"Yes, Your Highness, I stand corrected. It is now the ***season*** for me to begin my greatest work, for the order of things on the Earth is just as I'd like it," the devil responded.

"So, you're here for no one specific. Interesting," the Commander replied.

"It seems as if a better strategy, given the advancements in their technology, would be to take a more ***collective*** approach."

"I see." The Commander sat up on the throne, straightened His back, and raised His head. "I'm not lacking confidence in those who give Me their allegiance. And..."

"Commander!" Michael, the seraph, began to protest. Michael, just like Gabriel, was one given to fighting and war, for it was within his very nature; however, unlike his closest seraphim, he had learned through experience not to get so worked up and now exhibited the kind of emotional intelligence that lent itself well to leading many legions of fighting angels. At this moment, nevertheless, he could no longer withhold or maintain a sense of neutrality. He knew what Lucifer was requesting could be the beginning of an all-out war.

"No, no, it's fine. As I have said, I am confident those who give Me their ultimate allegiance will meet any new challenges with great fervency, regardless of whatever this villain throws at them. Lucifer, whatever it is you intend to do as you have described it this hour, you have my permission."

There was a gasp amongst those in the inner courts.

Lucifer's eyes narrowed, and he gave off a devilish smile. "Easier than I thought! But You just watch; You take away everything Your so-called followers have, and every last one of those Earth Dwellers will curse you to your fa—"

"But," the Commander interjected before Lucifer could finish, "you must divulge these plans ***before*** you administer them. To the Earth Dwellers."

"I will not. An impossible and implausible request. I refuse," Lucifer responded.

"Then you do not have my permission. Out of my sight. Michael, remove this degenerate from My presence," the Commander shot back, turning His head, waving His hand, and crossing His legs.

Michael moved forward, placing his enormous hands onto the devil. The devil wiggled his arms free before Michael could fully arrest him.

"Wait, wait. Forgive me." Lucifer at once took to a knee and carefully bowed his head. "What I meant to say, Your Highness, was, how are little old me and my team of little old men supposed to accommodate such a grand request? The Earth is so big, and we are so small in comparison. Marvelous, Your Highness, are the works of Your hands. Marvelous they are, indeed."

At that moment, the Commander paused and then waved for Gabriel to come forward. By this time, Gabriel was chomping at the bit. He was ready for war.

"Gabriel, remain calm. We received a handful of petition requests just a bit ago from several Earth Dwellers, did we not?"

In the blink of an eye, Gabriel was at the feet of the throne. "Chief, Your Highness, at Your request, I shall remain calm. And yes, we did." Gabriel answered attentively.

"And what were the contents? What were the Earth Dwellers asking for?"

"Well, Your Majesty, there are quite a few, but I have categorized them as best I could." Gabriel pulled out a handful of papers and began thumbing through them. "We had several health-specific requests, some urgent, some not. We have several Earth Dwellers needing to pay their bills and the rent, some others seeking Your help who are facing various financial challenges, like sudden eviction. There were a few asking for the deaths of those they hate, which I ***personally*** would not respond to, as I assume they may have confused this address for Your adversaries. Then, there are several others asking for some type of sign to prove that You are real, most of whom, if I may add, You have already granted such signs to before."

"That's it?" the Commander asked. "Anything else?"

Gabriel thumbed through the papers, throwing them to the ground, searching ardently for something that would put his Commander at ease. He froze as he looked over the last sheet.

"There is one more, Chief. A very specific one that could not be categorized."

"Well, what is it? What is the Earth Dweller requesting?"

"This request is of a different kind. The Earth Dweller is eagerly seeking You, and it seems his heart is content in simply knowing more about You, understanding Your ways, Your nature, and Your character," Gabriel said.

"He didn't ask for healing?"

"No, Commander. He didn't ask for healing."

"He didn't ask for money?"

"No, Chief, he didn't ask for wealth or prosperity, either."

"Very nice. Well, what is it? What is he wanting?"

"He is requesting that he be shown the things and events that will happen in the future. His request is very specific, I might add."

"Ah, he is asking to know My will for the Earth."

"Yes, it appears so, Chief."

"Very good." The Commander's demeanor changed in that moment to one of delightedness. "Lucifer, I believe we have found your accommodation," the Chief said, smiling. "Prepare yourself and your minions to go down to earth, you weasel."

Chapter 2

Earth

—

December 9, 2019

The time is of great importance. It is December 9, 2019, a day that will remain etched upon the pages of my mind as long as the cords of memory and time will lengthen. Quietly, I sit in my upstairs office, my desk neatly perched carefully against the wall. I breathe deeply, exhaling slowly and turning my head so that I might get a good view from my window into the warm and vibrant evening sky. The light from the neighbor's brick columns adjacent to my house has just flickered on, illuminating its soft and elegant beauty that punctures straight through the encroaching darkness around it. It is in this quiet moment that I am reminded of this thought: ***Light is to darkness what love is to fear; in the presence of one, the other disappears.*** As I ponder this thought, my right hand remains delicately draped upon my desk, and my fingers dribble up and down so carefully as I revel at the world beyond me. Shortly after, I see a tiny, speckled cat scamper across the empty street—frightened by the sudden sound of a barking dog just off into the distance.

Let me explain why I am writing this, and more importantly, why I am here.

You see, it is the eve of a very important birthday, my birthday, and at this particular moment, I have found myself in a deep and confounding rut of sorts, wondering what steps lie ahead in the winding staircase of my life. Perhaps, you, the reader, have at some point experienced such a feeling. Perhaps, like me, you have found yourself at one time or another alone at the doorstep of utter silence contemplating what paths may lie ahead.

The questions are likely similar. What possibilities of life lie before me? What will the remaining pages of my life contain? Will it be a wonderful work of drama or a timeless allegory? Will it be a warning or foreshadowing for others? Will it be a story of triumphant achievement and victory? Perseverance and overcoming?

Perhaps, it may be all these things; or perhaps, it may be none. Perhaps, there will be conquest; perhaps, there will be defeat. Perhaps, there will be tears of joy; perhaps, some tears of sorrow. Perhaps, there will be some right; perhaps, there will be some wrong. Will it be a perfect candle shining atop a hill or one that was quickly diffused into the ground? Infamy or honor? Esteem or disfavor?

At this moment, I am desiring a small glimpse into the depths of my future. I am salivating for some understanding of what the world will be, what my life will be, and what will eventually be and become of my earthly destiny. It's possible you have thought such thoughts yourself; in fact, I am confident and know that in this regard, I am not alone.

Over time, I have realized that I cannot blame anyone else or any other thing for the world that I live in, and along those same lines, I am well aware of the failures and shortcomings I have accumulated over the years. In this world and in this universe, I have come to see every human being as an intricate piece of the whole and each man's part in the unfolding drama as having utmost importance. Like a giant puzzle, at this particular moment in time, we can safely say that all of us and our pieces fit into this big world house and find our existence in this residence in our own unique way.

But just as it may be that we'll have a part to play in piecing together this giant puzzle, it is abundantly clear we sometimes cannot find where a particular piece or two fits into the grand scheme of the finished product as a whole. That is where I find myself on this day. That is where, I believe, the world finds itself in this season. Not a small number go around, day after day, attempting to piece together why exactly they have been placed here, for they ask such questions like these: "Who am I?" "Why am I here?" "Where did I come from?" And, "How important am I and my fellow man?"

It seems that in this time, on this eve as I pen these words, the world has been caught up in a web of disarray and finds itself incurable—trouble running rampant in the land with confusion all around.

There is darkness before us, and even deeper darkness rooted within us. A futile sense of nothingness seems to be clouding the skies of our personal world and our corporate world as well. This darkness has gripped men and women with unparalleled fears, sending them spiraling down the long corridor of crippling hopelessness and despair. ***And yet, I've heard it said that light is to darkness what love is to fear; in the presence of one, the other disappears.***

With that in mind, as I sit here, I find myself thinking intensely on the following possibility: Suppose I could think any thought or dream any dream that my heart so earnestly desires. Suppose I could use that ability to see into the future 5, 10, or perhaps even 50 years from now. Suppose I could ask any question and get any answer regarding the future and the destiny of every being and every creature that graces every crevice and sphere of this world. A secret, perhaps, to help those currently living and those who will one day inhabit planet Earth live a life free from the oppression and the hopelessness that has seemingly come to torture and torment so many in our days.

Let me stop supposing for just a second and again resettle toward the present truth. The truth of the matter is, like so many others, I have tried and tried, searching for answers via the readily available avenues of my day. The so-called "big names" and even those considered the "world's influential" don't seem to have them. A long look at the who's who in society will only assist in affirming this assessment. Yes, I've looked high, and I've looked low. I've looked near, and I've looked far. But no man thus far has been able to paint a sufficient picture of what the future of this world will hold and how

I and others must prepare for it. Things are changing around us at warp-like speed. If one simply turns on the television and skims the evening news, he will soon find that even these so-called "experts" are completely and absolutely delusional of what challenges or triumphs lie ahead. Thus, all of us find ourselves on a dangerous roller coaster ride, one spiraling out of control into utter darkness, propelling us passengers into many thousands of different directions, bringing about an awareness that soon the end may near, but yet we're so out of control that we simply hold on for dear life. ***But yet, even yet, light is to darkness what love is to fear; in the presence of one, the other disappears.***

In this moment of reflection, something wonderful has begun to happen. As I sit here alone, my mind suddenly begins to slow down, to ease.

You see, this aloneness affords no sound, and all I find in my possession, the only weapons at my disposal, are my thoughts. In the preceding years, if I have learned a thing, it is that in times of confusion and chaos, my life demands such silence. This time is one of those times. I have come to believe that it is my Father's way of whispering, "Son, it's time to get away." So, like a little child, I obey, going off to be alone to tap into the benefits of such solitude, void of all distraction of sorts. With me is no television, no phone, no music, nothing. And then, with time, the mental war ends, and the mind begins to quiet. I am left with the steady sound of my thoughts, my greatest weapons.

Let us return again to supposing. A few ticks pass, and I proceed to talk to my Father, taking my questions to Him regarding the future, the next 5, 10, 50 years, inquiring as to what exactly it might hold. I gently inquire as to how I and others might assemble for it. After all, He created it, so surely He has within Him the answer. In my whisper, I am, in reality, begging for direction, just to hear a simple voice, an assurance, no matter how quiet that assurance might be.

An hour quickly passes, then two. I hear nothing, and so I continue peering out my window, watching the small feline prance its way across my yard. It's crazy, isn't it, talking to this Person I call Father. It seems to be an act of faith to even attempt to raise one's voice and to focus one's complete thought and attention on a Being that one cannot physically see, in hopes of hearing an answer in whatever form that might be. But when one is in need of answers, answers mere humans cannot provide, what else can one do?

There was once a collection of teachings penned by a 17th-century monk, where the central theme of his message was the development of the awareness of the presence of the Father in one's everyday life. The brother, observing nature in the winter, at one time saw a tree stripped of its leaves and considered that within a little time, the leaves would be renewed, and after that, flowers and fruit would appear. Through this observation, he received a high view of the providence and power of the Father, which deeply impacted his soul for the remainder of his earthly life.

In reflecting on this writing, I had made it a point over the preceding weeks to seek to develop this keen sense of the Father in my own life and throughout all my dealings. One of the spiritual maxims presented to assist in developing just that is the faithful practice of the Father's presence. This directs one to keep his gaze entirely fixed on Him in faith—calmly, humbly, and lovingly, without allowing the appearance of anxious thoughts or emotions. It was a great undertaking in a world of constant busyness and distraction, but one that I felt was very much necessary, especially as I hoped to receive the guidance I so desperately longed for to assist in the focus and aim of my life as a whole. In essence, as I understand it, this maxim demands extended periods of silence in order to redirect and fix one's gaze on Him, and Him alone.

I would be dishonest if I told you this practice and this season had not been full of a few sleepless nights, many unanswered questions and a flood of doubts and fears. On this particular evening, unsure of how to proceed out of this stillness, supposition, and constant whispering to the Father, I again focus my attention on the desk and work before me and pull from my drawer a pen and sheet of paper. I begin to write out a letter with a list of questions that I would love for my Father to answer. I write as if the Father Himself were coming by to inquire of it that evening. I write freely but specifically until my stamina is diminished, my fingers are weak, and I can write no more. The entire process takes just shy of an hour from start to finish. Then, after a brief review, I carefully fold the document and place it directly in my drawer, handing it off to the Father in an act of simple faith. I had never done so with such great intention in the past before.

As you may have guessed, and to my disappointment, nothing particularly special happened that evening—or so I thought. It wasn't until a later occurrence, one I still cannot explain, took place early the morning of December 31, 2019, three weeks after I had penned that detailed letter, that I saw the significance of that night unfold. I recall the morning very clearly, for it had been another rather sleepless night, the third in a row to be exact, and I was disgruntled once again about the lack of clarity on the world and the direction of my future. This was exacerbated by the fact that in just a few hours' time, I would be celebrating the ringing of the new year, the new decade. Honesty again compels me to admit that I had forgotten about the details of the suppositions I had penned in the letter on the evening of that day, for I had not looked at it nor spoken of it since.

***

Now, before I continue further, let me pause for just a moment. I am asking that you read what follows very carefully, for to my knowledge, there has never been another who has had any such encounter. I would urge that you do not dismiss what is to follow as some sort of farce or extreme absurdity. I ask that you only consider it thoroughly with very careful and vigilant eyes.

Shall you agree? Yes? Let us now proceed.

At about 1:30 in the morning of the 31st, I heard an unceasing pounding on my door as I was finally dozing off to rest. As I sat up in my bed and listened, attempting to assure myself that I was not, in fact, dreaming, the pounding became louder and louder until finally, I was forced to lift myself from my position, put on my robe and slippers, and proceed to the entrance of my home. Turning on the porch light and looking through the peep, I saw a little tiny man with a clipboard standing just a few feet away. Behind him was a goliath of a man, whose head nearly touched the ceiling of my porch. This man could have been no shorter than about seven feet tall. He had on brown slacks and a blue knee-length coat.

I carefully opened the door slightly and inquired of both men. The short and stocky man standing in the front answered simply, "I have been sent by my Adversary as a response to your suppositions."

I asked the man plainly, "Who is your Adversary?"

At that, the man gave a quick and terse response, stating, "The One who governs the light."

The giant of a man behind him looked directly down at him and then up at me, nodding in approval. As he said this, the stocky man pointed to each of the various light fixtures in the neighborhood, from my night post to the light poles that lined the street neighborhood.

As the man was pointing, turning his head and hand in the direction of the night, I took a quick glance at his uniform—he wore a jet-black polo and kept a tiny pen fastened in his ear. His face was smooth and soft, graced with baby-like features. There appeared, at surface level, to be an innocence about him that made him seem somewhat shy. Before he turned to me again, I was able to glance at the tag on his shirt that I assumed bore the man's name. The name tag read simply, "Mr. 'Asbeel' Prince."

Asbeel, I immediately pondered to myself; however, I held my face calm as the man turned to me again.

"I see," I said to him, my eyes squinting, shaking my head in agreement. I began to probe for more. "This Man that governs the light… what suppositions did He receive from me that He has sent you to respond to at such a late hour as this?"

The short, stocky man by the name of Asbeel lifted his clipboard, flipped through a number of pages, and removed a sheet with several bullet points scribbled down upon them. He handed me the text, and I looked it over as he stood there, watching me in the night.

Indeed, the questions he had written were the questions I had been pondering and wrestling with personally for some time and then penned on the eve of my birthday, but they were nothing I had told to another. Yet even my name, number, and address were carefully inked on the paper.

I took my eyes again out to the street, this time to attempt to locate the stocky man's vehicle. Parked about a hundred feet down the road sat a small van, and on its side, it read in simple letters, "Prince of the Air."

"Is that your vehicle?" I asked. The stocky man nodded.

I looked at both the round little fellow and the goliath of a man behind him. My rational senses poured over me, and I quickly returned to consciousness. "It's 1:30 in the morning. Could you please come back tomorrow? I'd be happy to accommodate you then," I politely asked.

The man's face suddenly soured. "Unfortunately, I cannot," he said. "I have other business to attend to. Business, I might add, that will be affecting the entire globe."

Suspicious of what he meant and finding the statement somewhat strange, I looked the man over one last time. I began to move my cellular device from my pocket, deciding to call the local authorities for assistance, for I sensed a hint of deception, craftiness even, in the man's voice. Just as I did this, the hulking man behind him calmly stepped forward, moving the stocky man aside.

"Sir," he began. He immediately held out his hand, fingers stretched, cocked at an angle. I looked at it for a moment and then extended my own in return.

The moment our hands embraced, I felt a surge of power flow through me that I cannot describe. It felt as if a bolt of electricity had begun coursing through my veins, going down into my spine and simmering in my legs. At that moment, it strangely felt as if my body were receiving a recharging of some sort, as if my limbs had been plugged into some type of electrical outlet for the first time in a long time. Indeed, I began feeling things I had not felt in many years—an immensely strong and calming sense of peace and assurance, combined with exceptional power and strength. The anxiety and fear that had been haunting my days over the past several weeks quickly began to subside as I held the man's hand. I continued gripping it for some time. Both he and I said nothing.

"Come inside," I said as I flicked on the house lights. ***What an unusual experience***, I thought. However, I kept on, inviting the two men into my home with no real reason why except for the calming presence of the man whose hand I had just shaken. If it were not for his magnetism, I would not have agreed to let the two gentlemen inside. I, at once, folded up my phone and slid it back down into my pocket. My body was in a trance-like state, still feeling the effects of the handshake with the goliath of a man.

I quickly took the men into my dining area and pulled out two other chairs to allow them to be seated. At that point, as the two made their way to the chairs laid before them, Asbeel darted toward the light switch and quickly flicked it off. At once, the room was in complete and utter darkness, except for the flicker of streetlight that provided a small ray of illumination throughout the room. As the three of us stood there, in the darkness, an eerie coldness came over my body. I felt as if someone or something had begun to slowly suck the very life from within me.

Then, another strange thing transpired. Because the room was still dimly lit, I could see that the short, once stocky man had become larger. As a matter of fact, he appeared to be growing with each passing second in the darkness. He became so big that he now looked to be as large as the hulk of the man standing next to him. At that moment, I found myself unable to think clearly, unable to form a cohesive thought. My mental faculties were in complete and utter disarray.

It was a strange occurrence to be in such a state, but before it could last any longer, the giant man with the calming presence quickly stepped toward the wall and forcefully switched the lights back on. The room was again flooded with light, even brighter than it had been before, it seemed. The eerie feeling I had felt in the darkness slowly began to subside. Oddly, the short, stocky man who had appeared to have grown in the darkness returned to his regular size. Surely, some kind of trick was being played on my eyes. Nevertheless, my clear mental thinking began to return once more, and I continued toward my seat.

As we sat down at the table, I asked the stocky man if he preferred to be called by anything for short, as a nickname to Asbeel, to which he quickly shook his head "no."

"But I do prefer to have the lights off, if you don't mind," he added, his eyes squinting against the light. I pretended not to hear him, as the request seemed very odd. The man was so short that his feet dangled from the floor. He looked at me again and repeated his request—this time with more force.

"I prefer to have the lights off, ***if you don't mind***," he said again. I paused, thinking once more as to how I could accommodate the request. I then turned my attention to the large man next to him and curiously asked him his name.

"Michael," he replied.

"Michael. Great. Do you oblige if we honor this man's request?"

Michael shook his head. It was the most movement I had seen from him up until that time. "As long as I am here, the lights will remain on, thank you," he stated as he took his gaze directly to Asbeel. "If the soul is left in darkness, sins will be committed," he added.

What an odd thing to say. Without really understanding the statement, I nodded in approval and then posed my next question to both men.

"Would you care for anything to drink? Perhaps a cup of tea?" I had not the slightest idea what such men as these would prefer for a beverage.

"My only objective here," the stocky man said, "is to answer the questions within this letter, per the request of my Adversary."

"The Governor of the Light?"

"That is correct."

"Okay," I responded. I waited for a moment; however, Michael did not answer, so I averted the question. "Well then, let's not waste any more time. Let's get right to it." I briefly looked over the sheet he had handed me as one other very basic question came to mind.

"Any objection to the recording of this meeting?" I inquired of both men.

Michael turned to me and nodded "yes" in approval. "If that will help you recall our conversation, by all means, please do."

"Very well," I said. I placed my recorder on the table, hit the red button, and inched it a bit closer to both men. I then leaned forward in my own chair, preparing to pepper the man by the name of Asbeel first with the questions from the sheet.

What followed, I must say, was an utterly incredible conversation, at least in my own subjective opinion. I wish others, like you, could have been there. I have typed and formatted our engagement below so as to be easily legible by you and others interested in its contents.

Before you turn this page and begin reading the interview beginning with the man by the name of Asbeel, I should add that the legitimacy of the stocky man and the titan of a man is of little-to-no importance to me and should not be to you. Perhaps I am a victim of the effects of either habitual daydreaming or sleep deprivation, for I must admit, given my poor sleep history, I have not been immune to such in the past. What is important, however, is both men's prediction and analysis of their impact on the world and the stocky man's agenda in the world events to come. Both men provided a thorough assessment of the very questions I posed to my Father on the night of December 9, 2019.

Many, after reading it, may ask, "Is the text below simply a concoction of your imagination?" That I do not know. What I do know, however, and what I can say for sure, is that I vividly recall a very interesting conversation with the two men, one who specifically described himself as an adversary to the "Governor of the Light." It is very much a worthwhile read, and perhaps, it might prepare you for the age and season that is to come, as it has for me.

For light is to darkness what love is to fear; in the presence of one, the other disappears.

Chapter 3

Transcript of Interview with Asbeel, "Prince of Air"

—

Whereupon the following proceedings were in the dining room of my home, in the city of Boise, the early morning of December 31, 2019, and were transcribed late afternoon on December 31, 2019.

APPEARANCES:

Ebenezer O. Makinde
Asbeel, "Prince of Air," aka "Mr. Prince"
Michael, "Chief Archangel of the Heavenlies," aka "Michael"
Official Court Reporter: None

PROCEEDINGS

Ebenezer: Well, good evening, Mr. Prince. I have chosen to call you Mr. Prince. Do you oblige?

PRINCE: Hello. Good evening. For the sake of this interview, whatever you choose to call me is of little importance. Many people call me and my wonderful master by many different names, but regardless, our job and mission remain the same—because we are one...

(Pause)

PRINCE: Is it me, or is it bright in here? Why not dim the lights just a bit, shall we?

Ebenezer: Ok… excellent. I shall ask you concerning the mission you reference later. And I am sorry, but I, too, like Michael, would prefer that the lights remain on. Nevertheless, you have indicated that you are prepared and ready for the interview, so we shall proceed. The first question I have for you is this: Please explain to me in detail the reason for your presence here this evening.

PRINCE: I, specifically, am here at the request of my Adversary. I had no choice if I was to be permitted to bring about what I've been commissioned by my master to induce in your society in the coming months. My plans will soon be impacting every crevice of your earthly globe. Very well, perhaps the darkness will become more appealing to you at another time.

(Pause)

Ebenezer: Okay… could you please first begin by… (cough) first, begin by explaining to me the major differences between yourself and your Adversary?

PRINCE: The major difference between my Adversary and myself is that first and foremost, my master has at his control the systems of this world, as we currently know it. My Adversary rules the light, and I help rule the darkness. Both light and darkness, my Adversary and I exist in the world system—which you and your people call Earth. Other than that, our missions are the same.

Ebenezer: Thank you, Mr. Prince. When you speak of these systems, which systems are you referring to specifically? Please name them.

PRINCE: I refer to all the systems that readily come to your mind. The banking system, the healthcare system, the financial system, the government and political system, and the entertainment system. These are the major world systems that currently encompass my mission, our mission—for I and my master are one.

Ebenezer: I see. And of these systems you speak of, which of these are you most fond of? And which do you possess the greatest degree of control and influence over?

(Extended Silence)

Ebenezer: Mr. Prince, did you hear what I said? Would you like me to repeat the question?

(Silence)

PRINCE: No, I've heard you. You will have to excuse me—these questions, I might say, are quite whimsical and redundant in nature, for my Adversary knows very well my tactics. Anyway, there are currently just under eight billion people that occupy any one of these systems on this planet you all call Earth. But it is only through a single system that I wield my greatest influence over all the others and the people within them.

Ebenezer: And which system is that, Mr. Prince?

PRINCE: Unfortunately, I don't believe that is one of the questions you are permitted by my Adversary to ask me, Mr. Ebenezer. Is it?

(Inaudible)

Ebenezer: Uh… You are correct, Mr. Prince. It is not.

(Pause)

Ebenezer: Then please tell me about this mission you speak of. The mission you and those you work with seek to accomplish.

PRINCE: Our mission, and even that of my Adversary, is simple. We seek to rule the masses through the indoctrination of principles. This is the crusade we constantly engage in.

Ebenezer: Mr. Prince, if I understand you correctly, your master and ultimate ruler is the devil himself, is that correct? And if you work on the side of darkness and your Adversary is the light, then you are at war with God? And your war is one of principles?

PRINCE: I would very much prefer that you stick with the list before you. Although I am under no obligation to answer this, your observation and conclusion are correct. My master and I are one. I work under the being that has waged war with God, and we are in battle over the principles that govern the systems of this world.

Ebenezer: How and why would war be waged over mere principles? What do principles have to do with ruling the systems within the kingdom of this world, as you speak of?

PRINCE: I see we are back on track—to the questions that have been permitted, that is. But it is because of the mistake made by my Adversary...

Ebenezer: Mistake?

PRINCE: Yes, mistake. His error involves the one thing that He cannot and does not control. The most dangerous gift my Adversary gave man is none other than the human will. My Adversary intended to use the free will etched into the mind of man to fulfill His purposes on your Earth; however, giving man the power of choice means that a man or woman can freely exercise that right—to choose.

(Pause)

Ebenezer: Did you just say that God Himself is at the mercy of His own decision? To provide the human race with the power of will?

PRINCE: You have heard me correctly. A silly mistake by my Adversary, if you ask me. This is an actual fact.

Ebenezer: And who would you claim is winning this war? This war between the darkness and the light?

PRINCE: Oh! How silly a question! I will answer you anyway since I am under orders by my Adversary to be under such catechism... but first, I will ask you this. Which humans control the spread of information in your world, and how do they go about executing that control?

(Pause)

Ebenezer: Well, any new event is covered and disseminated through the news by the various media outlets. Any time a new event happens, they gather the information and release their narrative.to the world

PRINCE: And why do they control the narrative?

Ebenezer: Well, Mr. Prince, I would have to say I do not know. Up to this time, I've never thought much about that.

PRINCE: I will tell you why. They control the narrative because it is the most effective medium for the proliferation and dissemination of my ideals. That is why the majority of our time in this war against light is spent maintaining control over the few mediums that ultimately shape and control the narrative that you Earth Dwellers consume. To you and other humans, it may appear that a large multiple of media companies influence this flow of information; however, this is not true. Even in this age of global connectivity, any medium that controls the distribution of information and the self-distribution of information can easily be silenced as long as I maintain a strong grip on the larger ones. With this, I control news stations, newspapers, publishing houses, Internet, utilities, videogame developers...

Ebenezer: Aha. So, it may be said that the entertainment medium *is* the channel by which your greatest influence and control over the masses is birthed.

(Extended Pause)

Ebenezer: Mr. Prince?

PRINCE: This is my response to your statement, a response I am offering out of my own selfish generosity. Many, many years ago, the war between my Adversary and I began when the will of man was appropriated for the first time. At that time, the thought of man was perfectly in line with my Adversary—whatever He communicated to him in the form of thought and information was received with all certainty to His apex of creation called man. At that time, my darkness had no control over any Earth Dweller; however, the capacity to receive darkness based on the mistake of my Adversary was still present—it had just not been activated. With only light for thought and as the sole source of information, everything that man did was without confusion, destruction, unpleasant emotion, or distress. It was a sick world, to say the least. His ability to create objects and artifacts that developed this planet in a healthy, orderly manner remained completely intact and was destined to expand, given the instruction by the Adversary to be fruitful, multiply, and fill the entire Earth. My Adversary enjoyed complete control over the heart and mind of man during that time. It was then that my team, headed by my master, sought to develop a plan to gain control of the man through the control of his thought.

Ebenezer: I understand. Thank you for such a thorough explanation. So, in short, you seek to control the thought of man through the control of principles disseminated through various mediums.

PRINCE: If I were to assess the accuracy of your statement, I would find no flaw within it. It seems you excel in dumbing down information—a great weapon for wielding influence over the masses. My master and I could use you. How about I give you my card, and we chat sometime later? The pay is quite handsome.

Ebenezer: I'm not in need of a new position, but thanks. Now tell me more about your group that rules the darkness. I'd like to know more. Please proceed.

PRINCE: Shucks. Well, fine. But to understand us, you must first understand the word "principle" and its meaning. The word is derived from the root word "prince," which simply means "first law." In this world which we seek to control, we operate under principles, or first laws, just as does our Adversary. For through the manipulation of this law, the dissemination of this distortion, and the consumption of it through various mediums by you humans, we are able to expand our kingdom. Our kingdom can be found wherever and through whomever—even those that choose not to acknowledge us! You have perhaps seen our kingdom in many places and in many forms, and it is evidenced by things like hatred, discord, jealousy, fits of rage, selfish ambition, dissensions, factions, envy, drunkenness, orgies, and sexual immorality. We specialize in and love disseminating "new" first laws throughout all our mediums related to these distorted principles. And we've found that they are readily accepted by many and covertly accepted by those who are unaware of our tactics. Very few find themselves uninfluenced by our control.

Ebenezer: These very few, the ones that remain uninfluenced by your control... who are they? And by the way, your kingdom, as you've described it, is one that I am, in fact, aware of—if it truly is as you've described it.

(Silence)

Ebenezer: Mr. Prince, Michael is ***not*** a part of this interview, and he cannot answer or speak for you, so please turn both your attention and eyes to me and address me only, for I am not finished with your questioning.

PRINCE: Lower your tone with me, Ebenezer, or I will have you crawling in no time through the use of my tactics like an ailing, sick dog—tail between its legs. ***Remember, my master and I are one.*** Who are they that remain uninfluenced by my control, you ask? Those that pledge their full allegiance to my Adversary, not in word, but in action and deed as well. For those who express their allegiance only through creed are some of my greatest instruments for furthering and expanding my control over your earthly systems. Those who find themselves free from my control accept and guard the principles given by my Adversary, principles by which I have put all my effort into distorting or controlling. These men represent the repulsive principles of love, joy, peace, patience, kindness, goodness, faithfulness, gentleness, and self-control. Under these principles, my many tricks and tools are made to be of little-to-no effect. However, as I have stated, the scale has and will continue to tilt in my favor. In the favor of my master's kingdom and not theirs.

Ebenezer: Mr. Prince… Mr. Prince, as I said before, please address ***ALL*** of your responses to me and not to Michael, for I am the one conducting this interview, and I am the one you must respond to. I am not afraid of you, and I will speak to you as I please. Now, will you further tell me about your tactical, operational strategy for the expansion of your kingdom?

PRINCE: Hmm, no fear, huh? I don't believe it in even the slightest. To understand my tactical strategy, you must look at it in its simplest form, when my master first deployed it with the first man and woman many, many years ago. It is a very straightforward strategy, I might add. As I have stated, he simply took the original principle given by my Adversary and reintroduced it to man in a slightly altered form. With his craftiness and persuasion, man believed it. Doing so that first time was fairly easy, but had it not been accepted, my master and I would have repeated, repeated, and repeated the distortion of the original principle until it was. Eventually, my master and I would have had our way with man. ***Eventually***, we would have gained complete, uninhibited control over man's thought pattern or belief.

Ebenezer: Okay… (inaudible). It appears that belief by your victim is important to your success, if not your ultimate goal. Define belief as you see it, for it appears this may be the tipping point in the battle against your Adversary for these earthly kingdoms you speak of.

PRINCE: By this interrogation, or whatever you might call it, you are exposing my master's greatest secret—my greatest secrets, for as you know, my master and I are one. I understand why my Adversary has forced our representation here. You say you're not afraid, but you are only quite lucky that Michael is here to protect you. Or else you, my friend, would undoubtedly be the next victim of my tricks. As a matter of fact, I renege on the previous offer. I don't believe you are fit at this present time to take any responsibility from me, let alone my master. But I will begin answering your question by first making this statement: There is no way to violate a principle made by my Adversary and survive. We that rule the darkness live by, operate by, and wage war by this rule. Belief is nothing but a man's conviction. My goal, as I have stated, is to inundate individuals with new first laws that are against my Adversary's. It is my goal to not let a man think how my Adversary believes he is supposed to think, or else my fellow comrades and I will fail. So how do I do this? I keep the chains on their minds and change their beliefs one small precept and principle at a time. I have workers in all systems of the world that are there to distract the masses through the dissemination of principles that are counter to the light. As a man thinks in his inner mind, so he is. The inner mind is the one below the conscious mind. A man is whatever he believes to be in his inner mind. If I can control the inner mind of the human, I have won. I control the mind below the conscious mind by working on the conscious mind first, and I simply keep repeating,

repeating, repeating, and repeating until the conscious mind deposits my principles into the man's inner mind. It is a wonderful thing when I see a man finally begin to unconsciously act out things like murder, lust, and adultery and not even be aware of it or be convicted by it. That is when I, my master, and his forces, have won.

Ebenezer: Mr. Prince, I am becoming a bit disturbed by this confession.

(Pause)

Ebenezer: But I suppose I must go on. What other ways do you change beliefs, seeking to alter the inner mind, other than through traditional media as the Earth now uses it? And can you please give us an example of a prototype victim?

PRINCE: You should not be disturbed. ***I only offer the truth, the real truth; remember that anything else other than this truth is only a threat to your freedom.*** Freedom that my Adversary seeks to take away. I have every medium through every world system at my disposal to change beliefs. I use parents, friends, relatives, acquaintances, public and private figures–anything that can communicate information through the various airwaves. Over the last 30 or so years, the Internet has become a wonderful tool for such dissemination. That is where I specialize. I was able to worm my way into getting control of it by using the tactics I just mentioned on the various people groups. Very soon, my ideals and beliefs will become new first laws in even the underdeveloped nations and countries, such as Nigeria, Zambia, and Burundi.

Ebenezer: So global expansion is a part of the agenda, I see.

PRINCE: Is your water wet? Is your sky blue? Absolutely. Global expansion *is* the agenda. In fact, it may already be too late for anyone looking to stop me from spreading my master's ideals throughout the entire world. The technological advances in recent years have made my work much easier. As you can see, I've even put on a few pounds because of it.

Ebenezer: Hmm… I've never found it too late for even the most difficult of changes to take place. Of that, I remain optimistic. But very well. Let's circle back once again to your prototype victim. Who is he, and what are your tactics for gaining your control over him?

PRINCE: Oh yes, my prototype victim. Ideally, I would like to introduce my principles to you earthly beings during the early period of your earthly development. I have found that this is difficult with those people who have the stability of a healthy family, for that, in itself, is a major principle of my Adversary. So, I prey on broken families, where the parents are absent, either physically or emotionally, and the children are left to fend for themselves. I love any type of division within the home. My success rate in these types of scenarios is very, very high, for obvious reasons.

Ebenezer: I am a bit confused and don't understand why this would be so obvious?

PRINCE: Mr. Ebenezer, you are once again asking questions that go beyond the scope of this interview or interrogation, whatever we are to call it. But nevertheless, because I am feeling a bit munificent at this moment, I will tell you a short story, a glorious story, about a boy that I recently took control of… let us begin. As the wonderful story goes, there was a young boy about the age of 11 who lived in a large family. The family, although the parents were still together, was emotionally isolated from one another and usually kept issues and problems to themselves. The mother suffered from a deep and crippling anxiety, and the father worked tirelessly, day and night, ***chasing the allure of the dollar***. He failed to ever develop any emotional connection with his children. This type of victim is oh-so-ripe for my taking. And so, when the young boy began to hear, see, and listen to the principles I had been spreading through the mediums I control, he had no other choice but to accept what I was feeding him. He had no buffer for this information, and he wasn't receiving enough of the original principles from my Adversary, even though he and his family attended religious services and even were members of religious organizations. So, after a year's time of repeating, repeating, repeating, and repeating my principles, they were deposited and downloaded into the boy's inner mind, and I now, to this day, have him under my control.

Ebenezer: So, isolation aids in your cause?

PRINCE: ***Absolutely***. Think back to the first man and woman and the tricks I played on them. Isolation and independence are fertile ground for ***all*** my endeavors.

Ebenezer: You are crafty, indeed. What is it about isolation and independence that is so critical to your cause?

PRINCE: Without "healthy" family, as my Adversary sees it, there is no mission. And where there is no mission, there is no identity. And where there is no identity, a person becomes open to taking on the identity placed on him by other people through various other mediums. Social groups, social clubs, congregations, political parties, online groups, gyms, fan clubs, religions, which the latter, I may add, are by far my favorite—the list goes on and on. But the fact remains that all of these are new identities that are readily at my disposal. For example, in the story I told you about the 11-year-old, his parents, brothers, and sisters did not help him to define his mission and identity within the larger mission of the family under the guidance of my Adversary's original laws. Rather, he went to other sources and other mediums and people I control to ***tell him who he is***. That's ***exactly*** where I want him—having other people under my control defining what and who he should be. It's a recipe for a very wonderful disaster.

Ebenezer: Mr. Prince, is there any way, once this disaster, as you call it, happens, to reverse the effects of it?

PRINCE: No. No. NO. I will NOT speak of this.

Ebenezer: Mr. Prince, the question is right here...

(Silence)

PRINCE: (Sigh) Whose grand idea was this paper anyway? Well, I suppose I have no choice. This is a very good question, and I ***hate*** it. But nevertheless, many of my victims, usually years after I first take control of their inner minds, wonder desperately why they try to follow my Adversary but are unable to do so faithfully. Sometimes, I pity them. But then I remember my Enemy, and this feeling of solace soon leaves me. There are two remedies that I have seen one caught up in my clutches use to free himself. To explain each effectively, please allow me to communicate in technical computer terms: if incorrect software has been downloaded onto the hard drive of a computer, how does one clean the hard drive and remove the things that had been previously downloaded? Sometimes, one must buy a brand-new computer with a brand-new hard drive because what has been downloaded is so heavily ingrained into the system. Or, as is usually the case for my victims, one must buy another program that literally works to clean the old system out. My Adversary has such software to do this, and that is to His major advantage in this war. There. Is that not what you want to hear? It is my understanding that it is readily available to all who ask. But often, this is not the simple fix that you Earth Dwellers search for, and so you decide you'd rather hide the fact that your hard drive is completely corrupted, rather than deal with it and address it head-on. Do as you wish with this information.

Ebenezer: I'll have to think on this later…

PRINCE: I wouldn't advise you to do so for too long. It is only by force that my Adversary has coerced me into divulging what I have just shared with you. Remember, ***I myself only offer the truth, the real truth; anything else other than this truth is only a threat to your freedom.*** Freedom that my Adversary seeks to take away.

Ebenezer: Hmm. Understood, but for the sake of time, let's move on. Let's now retreat and discuss your prototype victim once again. Could you explain to me how this victim may go on in life, unaware of the effect that control over his inner man has done and where it is leading him?

PRINCE: Yes. I will gladly address my prototype victim further. This young boy will soon grow into adolescence, and he will likely choose a career path at that time. For the sake of this conversation, let's say this young man goes into one of my favorite systems—entertainment...

Ebenezer: Ah, so you are implying once again that the entertainment medium *is* your system of choice.

PRINCE: Mr. Ebenezer, I have not, and I will not confess to such a statement! Now, where was I... oh, yes. This newly minted adolescent has spent years and years being inundated with my principles since the early years of his childhood. They have now been deposited into his inner man, and they are running on his "hard drive" on autopilot. This young man still attends the weekly religious ceremonies where my Adversary is celebrated; however, it is clear to me that he still belongs to me and is under my control. Because I have been influencing his inner man for most of his life, I have succeeded in stripping him of his esteem, his personal value, and the unique identity that my Adversary had given him but has not had an opportunity to claim. Now, here comes the fun part. Through the work of the various systems of the world I control, I begin to flood ideas through the mediums my victim has grown accustomed to that make him believe that it is now time for him to choose a career path. I help him with that decision by giving him many different ideas and opinions from millions upon millions of people, who, I might add, are under my control and are living the lifestyle that appeals to what has already been downloaded into his inner man.

Ebenezer: It seems as if this is a lifelong process. One that begins at a point when many young children may not be able to even decide for themselves as to which influence, either yours or your Adversary's, the individual would like to be ruled under. In my opinion, that does not seem fair.

PRINCE: It is a good thing that your opinion means absolutely nothing! To me, at least. My focal concern is the destruction of my Adversary through the corruption of His principles and the gaining of control over the masses through the flooding of those principles through the mediums available within the systems I control. How is that for a mouthful? But you speak correctly; that it is a process that begins immediately from birth. I believe you Earth Dwellers call this "nurture." But those who follow me, who are under my control, get to experience all the wonderful things that define my kingdom, things my Adversary opposes, but things that bring you humans the greatest sensual pleasure. For I offer them an abundance of earthly power, an abundance of money, and a copious amount of sex. And if they obey me fully, I have at my disposal as much of it as they would like.

Ebenezer: But in the long run, Mr. Prince, it can be said that these things will eventually destroy the man if used under the altered principles that you have championed and enslaved them under.

PRINCE: Yes, that is my intention.

Ebenezer: Well, then, Mr. Prince, you are a very cunning and seditious man. What about men and women who ***do*** manage to "clean out their hard drive," as you speak of, and are no longer under the control of your influence?

PRINCE: Mr. Ebenezer, must we deal in such low-probability discussions? I have seen very few people become even the least bit effective again if I have them in my grasp and under my control from the time they are little. Even if they no longer live under the direction of my distorted principles, there is still one thing that I can use to keep them down, from completely being given over to my Adversary.

Ebenezer: And what is that, Mr. Prince?

PRINCE: You humans call it ***shame***. Shame is my weapon of choice for assuring that the future of my victims still remains securely fixated under my control. If they decide they no longer want to live under the influence of my principles, I immediately disseminate voices through my mediums confirming, affirming, and reaffirming to them that they are undoubtedly a mistake and that they ought to be ashamed for even allowing themselves to be under my influence for any amount of time. I tell them over and over and over again that they have no reason for hope and that there is nothing in life for which to be joyful. This is one of my favorite little tricks once my control on them begins to loosen. Yes, they may spend eternity with my Adversary, but my primary goal is to destroy their lives here on Earth and sabotage their potential and their minds so I can maintain unadulterated control.

(Silence)

Ebenezer: Mr. Prince, it appears we are now at a shift in the conversation, which is good because I will readily admit I will need some time to digest this. You seem to have some deep-seated anger that you have yet to address publicly as well. But I digress. The current date is December 31, 2019. We are just a day from the beginning of the coming year. What plans do you have going into the new decade?

PRINCE: My plans for the new decade are the same as that of the last. Mr. Ebenezer, are you paying any attention to the responses I am giving you? Or am I wasting my time here? I have work in the world that my master has assigned me that eagerly awaits to be done.

Ebenezer: Mr. Prince, let me remind you, I am simply reading from the script provided to me by your Adversary.

PRINCE: But, but, but my presence here is a response to your request.

Ebenezer: I suppose.

PRINCE: I suppose as well.

Ebenezer: Well, as you have previously stated, you have no alternative but to answer every question listed by your Adversary. Therefore,

I will take as much time as needed, and I will ask you again: What are your plans for this coming decade?

PRINCE: We seem to be becoming a bit bolder now, aren't we?

Ebenezer: As I have stated, I am not afraid of you, nor your master. Now, answer my question.

PRINCE: Ha! If it weren't for Michael here, I would already have you within the clutches of my influence. You haven't seen even a smidge of my anger yet. And speaking of influence, I must say it's still a bit too bright in here—shall we turn down the lights? What is it that you do again?

Ebenezer: I am currently employed within the banking industry. I work for one of the largest community banks on the West Coast. And, no, as I've stated before, the lights shall remain on for the remainder of this discussion.

PRINCE: Ah, the banking system! You don't strike me as the type. Nevertheless, I must say, it's fairly easy to gain control over that system. And fine—suit yourself.

Ebenezer: Is that a system you are actively seeking to take over as well?

PRINCE: Seeking? That system currently ***is*** under my control. It didn't take much effort, I should add, for the distortion of the proper use of money, and the love of that money has given me easy access into that world. My time, therefore, is better spent trying to gain stronger control over other systems… you used the word "currently." What is it that you have always wanted to do? What is your deepest desire?

Ebenezer: Interesting. As I think about it, all decisions ***are*** decided based on the bottom line, and it causes people to do fascinating things. But to answer your question, I've always wanted to be in the entertainment industry—writing, producing, and hosting film and television productions. I have desired it ever since I was a child. I've done a few projects here and there so far, but nothing more.

PRINCE: Don't worry; you have the time. Don't be afraid to ***enjoy*** what you're doing for a few more years before giving that your full attention. Time is on your side. Time is on your side. Again, I say ***time is on your side***. Anyway, let us return to your question. What is it you ask again?

Ebenezer: Your plans, Mr. Prince. Your plans. What are your plans for the coming decade?

PRINCE: Oh, yes. My plans. I will present my plans for the next decade in very simple, plain terms. I will be expanding my reach, of course. To say it to you plainly, I intend to get my hands into every good thing that still exists in you humans' lives. I will be looking for every opportunity to wiggle my way so deeply into your personal affairs so that I can walk off with everything you hold precious and dear. Once I have stolen all your goods and possessions, I will take my plan to rob you and your fellow earthlings to a greater level. My master and I intend, and have been granted full permission, to create a situation so horrible that you will see no way to solve the problem except to sacrifice and give up everything that remains. To say it more succinctly, I want to waste and devastate lives. And nothing will stop me. This decade, I will leave more and more people insolvent, broke, and cleaned out in every area of their lives. They will feel as if they are finished and out of business. I will completely obliterate them, creating a very dark and cold world.

Ebenezer: Mr. Prince, that is quite an impact on the decade you have planned. Up to this time, I have never really taken a moment to think about what ways you may be seeking to impact our daily lives. Behind the veil of your behavior, I sense there has to be a greater motive. What exactly is it that you want from us? What *is* your ultimate motive?

PRINCE: I will tell you what I want. I will divulge to you my ultimate motive. I desire for the goodness of evil to reign. And I want all men to see my master as he is and me as I am, as a being who is greater than my Adversary. I want complete and total worship. And I also, as I mentioned, want you to be utterly helpless and defeated. I want you to struggle through your entire life, only realizing at the end that my Adversary had made you for more. I can picture it now: men and women lying on their deathbeds, grasping for their last breath, bodies ravaged with sickness and ill health, wishing they could go back and relive their younger days, days they spent unknowingly sold out to me and my agenda. Yes, I want you to be so sick, so depressed, and so miserable that it keeps you occupied and in constant fear. I want you to feel like you will never hit the target with your life. And once your life is finished, I don't want anyone to even recognize that you are gone. I want my kingdom and my government to reign supreme throughout the face of the entire Earth. Yes, I want worship. Complete and total worship for myself and my master. How is that for a plan?

Ebenezer: Well, now I know, Mr. Prince, that you are truly vile and sinister in nature, for to destroy and snatch away the legacy of a man or woman so that they might be forgotten by all future generations is a terrible thing. I am sure that many unassuming, innocent people have suffered at your hands simply because they were unaware of the principles of truth. However, I do beg to dig a bit deeper and question you just a bit more, for your answer to me comes across as the result of a plan, but not the actions to bring about the result for which you seek. Please, tell me now so I might be aware: What is your plan?

PRINCE: You are quite intelligent, I can see. Are you sure the entertainment system is right for you? For many, that answer suffices and sends them into an immediate state of pandemonium, simply because they do not have the composure to sit face to face with me and probe for the truth. Although I am under no obligation by my Adversary to answer this question regarding my exact plans, I would encourage you to look through the last hundred or so years of the world's existence to see the pattern and rhythm that I religiously follow. Ah, religious… again, one of my favorite words. Anyway, perhaps in doing so, you will realize that it isn't so much what is done by me, but it is how what is done is reported, proliferated, disseminated—and the ending result.

Ebenezer: Hmm. In all the previous crises I can think of, there is only one thing I can find that was a common theme in all of them.

PRINCE: And what might that theme be?

Chapter 4

The Heavenlies

—

December 31, 2019

"Uriel… Uriel… would you please move just a little bit to the right?" Hadrenial, still the one manning the big pearly gates, begged. Uriel, who was beaming from ear to ear, looked over his shoulder but seemingly brushed Hadrenial's request aside.

"Did you hear me? For Commander's sake," he muttered under his breath. Deciding to pick up his clipboard and change his own position, he meandered a few feet to the right in order to avoid the bright rays coming directly from Uriel's aura. It was back to business as usual for all the angels-those who had come from Earth had now returned to their duties, and those who resided in the Commander King's country went back to their respective responsibilities of ensuring that the Heavenlies functioned and operated as expected. The devil and his minions, it was well understood, were somewhere on Earth, fulfilling the request of the Commander to divulge all their secrets for the coming decade.

On rare occasions after such a big event, the Commander King would request that a few of the seraphim switch positions—some would take a new position closer to the throne, while others would be reassigned on special assignment to some deserving Earth Dweller, making it necessary to descend to Earth once more for various assignments. But to Hadrenial's dismay, not only had he ***not*** been assigned to a new position; he had actually been commended for his work during the big day all the angelic forces presented themselves before the Commander's throne. The way he handled Lucifer was especially commended. Therefore, the Boss asked that he remain right next to the big pearly gates and work with Uriel under the supervision of Saraqael as the gatekeepers who ushered every Earth Dweller with citizenship into the Heavenlies through the gates and into the new country.

The job was fairly straightforward. Each new permanent resident would be accompanied by their respective angel until they reached the top of the ladder. They would first check in with Saraqael, who, on all occasions, would reach out for a hug and give the citizen a warmer-than-warm smile. Both he and Uriel, who was mainly there to add to the dramatic effect of entering the new country, would then brief them on the general protocols of resident life in the Heavenlies, something that no Earth Dweller ever seemed to really grasp but on seemingly all occasions, they nodded as if they did. Then, Uriel and Saraqael would move to the side, and it became Hadrenial's turn to review the book containing the chapters of their life and take the time to reflect on the work and assignments the individual had completed, or failed to complete, on Earth. He would sit there and check off box after box of the things that the Earth Dweller had been given to do prior to being deposited into the Earth. Even though he wasn't much of a fan of standing for extended periods of time, he did find it somewhat interesting reviewing what each Earth Dweller had accomplished, or did ***not*** accomplish, during their sojourn on Earth.

For some time, Saraqael had been pacing slowly up and down but suddenly stopped and turned his shoulders, pointing toward the ladder that started in the Earth, punctured the heavens, and stopped at the pearly gates.

"Looks like we got another," he said.

Hadrenial held tight to his clipboard and took a few steps forward to meet the newest member of the Heavenlies. The Earth Dweller, upon reaching the top of the ladder, moved slowly toward the gates, his eyes wandering to and fro, inspecting his new surroundings for the very first time. It was always a beautiful and perfect day in the Heavenlies, and this day was no different. A small patter of rain had just ceased a few moments before, and the wonderful aroma left in its wake was unlike anything any Earth Dweller could have experienced on Earth.

"Well, hello there," Saraqael said, extending out his angelic arms to give the man a hug.

"I'm here in Heaven," the man responded as he extended his own arms while continuing to admire his environment.

"You're here, indeed. Welcome to the Heavenlies, your new residence for the time being." The two embraced, and then Saraqael moved to the side to allow for Uriel to greet him and for Hadrenial to approach with his checklist.

"Mr. Bigsby, it's great to see you here. Welcome," Uriel said.

"Thank you," the man by the name of Mr. Bigsby repeated. "Is my wife here?" he asked, curiously turning to Hadrenial.

It was a question that the seraph knew was coming, for almost all new residents entering through the gates asked about one relative or another. It was a question especially relevant for Mr. Bigsby, who, at the age of 45, had lost his wife in an accident. He himself was quite young, being only 55. Nevertheless, for dramatic effect, Hadrenial took his clipboard and ran his pen along the pages, stopping at a point at the very end of the text.

"Yep, looks like Mrs. Bigsby is here," he responded.

"Oh, thank God," he said.

"Yes," Hadrenial nodded, "you'll be able to thank Him in person soon. But first, let's take an inventory of your activity on Earth."

Hadrenial began to look over the man's assignments, the ones given to him to do on Earth. To his surprise, almost none of the boxes were checked. In other words, the man had accomplished very little of what the Commander had given him to do. Hadrenial's face soured.

"Mr. Bigsby, congratulations on making it here—we are very excited to have you. But it doesn't look like you were able to exercise all the gifts the Commander gave you and build some of the things He had put within you to do?"

Mr. Bigsby looked at Hadrenial with big eyes but said nothing. Hadrenial continued.

"With the incredible ability you were given to be able to see into the future as a man of great vision, combined with your love for business, I would have thought you'd have started a business using my Commander's principles that sought to not only make money but to give to those who were more so in need?"

Mr. Bigsby shrugged his shoulders.

"Well, I thought about that early in my career. But, you know, it was just too risky. The economy was so volatile, and financially, I just couldn't bring myself to putting up the money when I was younger. A lot of the money at the time was for my retirement, you know. And well, you know, things in the world over time just became more and more uncertain, and life happened, so it seemed better to just push forward and secure myself financially first. But I did try. At the age of 45, I gave up everything after Mrs. Bigsby died, and I made plans to begin giving it all away. I even put off much of the building of my house for it, which I never saw finished. But then the sickness and all that happened… and I just never got around to it. It was just too much risk… much too much risk early in my career. But I tried. And I'm here, right?"

Hadrenial nodded and scribbled down a few notes on his clipboard. Upon completion, he stepped to the side and opened the big pearly gates for Mr. Bigsby to enter.

"Yes, you are here. You did quite a bit in your lifetime, that's for certain. Valedictorian, double major, a budding philanthropist…"

The kind words made Mr. Bigsby smile. "Welcome to your new home," Hadrenial added warmly. "I'll have Netzach, my assistant here, meet you right inside to give you a tour of your new temporary home. Your new residence awaits, and there is much for you to do, Mr. Bigsby."

Slowly, the big, pearly gates expanded, and Mr. Bigsby calmly made his way inside.

Chapter 5

Earth

—

December 31, 2019

Ebenezer: The common theme in the previous crises seemed to be a lingering sense of fear that endlessly perpetuated itself and severely gripped the people's hearts and minds.

PRINCE: Ah, fear. Fear is the greatest tool at my disposal for the controlling of the masses, and it has become easier and easier over time to spread it throughout the world given the recent advancements in making people more connected. As I have told you, I already possess within my control the larger mediums that disseminate information to the masses. Of course, not all the information given by the systems I control is directly to my liking. However, in running my operation in that manner, I am able to strategically place various ideas and thoughts into the minds of humans that they more readily accept due to the trust I have built up with them over time. I am very excited for what I have in store for this decade; I will be able to reach more people than I ever have before in the shortest amount of time with what is coming in the near future. Even long after what I have planned is over, I shall have this world propagated with fear and erratic behavior, keeping it entrenched in the global psyche. Perhaps you remember the terror I unleashed on the world in 1345, the one nearly 100 years ago in 1918, the one 40 years ago in 1981, and the one you may have experienced in 2003. This time, the effects and aftereffects combined for what I have planned will be much more powerful given the increase in air travel and global connectedness.

Ebenezer: I now understand and can see how you have tactically wielded your influence over time. Perhaps many people beyond me will benefit from hearing this information. It seems as if the world, though it has more and more information concerning the patterns of history, has developed a sort of amnesia that only allows man to think in terms of the here and now and off into the future, but not so much of the past. Things happen, people ruminate on them for a few days, and then they move on. Is that how you see it, Mr. Prince?

PRINCE: Yes, and that, too, is to my advantage. I can feed a person with information from many different sources, similar in nature, and because of their forgetfulness and their short attention spans, it is as if I am presenting it to them for the very first time. All the while, I am working my philosophies and ideologies deeper into their inner mind.

Ebenezer: Mr. Prince, based on this statement, I must ask you a question concerning an issue that has been going on for quite some time here in my country. This question, however, is not on the list...

PRINCE: As I have stated, and as you know, I am under no obligation to answer it. However, out of my own curiosity, ask away, and perhaps, you may get lucky.

Ebenezer: That's exactly what I was hoping for, Mr. Prince. I'll try my luck. This question has to do with relationships between those of various people groups here in the United States. It seems that there is a struggle for some groups to gain the genuine respect of others. There seems to be a devaluation of even human life that permeates the interactions between these groups. I have yet to make up my mind definitely if this is true. What do you have to say to this? Is this of your doing? I believe I know the answer based on a few of your previous statements; however, I would like to hear it straight from your mouth.

PRINCE: I will respond to your question by saying this: My Adversary has His ideal for the family structure, and I have mine. My Adversary has His ideal for friendships, and I have mine. My Adversary has His ideals that He believes should govern all interpersonal engagements, and as you guessed it, I have mine. Do what you want with this information. However, that is as far as I will go and as much as I will give you concerning this topic. Perhaps there is some truth in your statement regarding the answer being embedded in the statements I have already made regarding my influence and control.

Ebenezer: Fine. Let's move on. Mr. Prince, you have told me much about your schematics for influencing the world; however, you have not spoken much about your Adversary up until this time other than your last statement. Although this list does not include much about Him, I ask that you allow me to pepper you with questions concerning His nature and intentions for mankind so I can get a better understanding of the relationship and constant differences between the two of you.

PRINCE: I have no desire to talk in detail about my Adversary. He works for Him; why not direct your questions to him?

Ebenezer: Michael, you work for his Adversary?

MICHAEL: Yes, I do. I currently lead…

PRINCE: Please, please. No need for a resume. Just on with the questions so I can get out of here and back to my work.

Ebenezer: Mr. Prince, your time has passed, and neither are you in control over the time and flow of this meeting. Thank you. Michael, please continue in telling me who you are.

MICHAEL: I'm Michael, the Chief Archangel of the Heavenlies. I lead and head the battalion of angels, answerable only to my Commander...

PRINCE: I am Miiii-chaellll, Archangel of the Hea-ven-lies… BLAH BLAH BLAH…

Ebenezer: Mr. Prince! Your time is up. Thank you. And why have you come here today? With him, Michael?

MICHAEL: Because the accuser and his men have no power except it be given to them by my Commander. My Commander has commissioned me to bring this weasel here to answer you on their behalf, upon your request. Your petition was received by the Heavenly Office on December 10, 2019, at 2:44 a.m.

Ebenezer: Very well. Yes, the timing is accurate. That was one of a string of sleepless nights, I do recall. And what do you say, Michael, to the prince's claims?

MICHAEL: I have nothing to say in regard to his efforts. What is done is done, and the battle has already been won. Yes, this man works for the most scrupulous liar that walks the face of the Earth, and we refrain from acknowledging even his presence, for again, whatever he is allowed to do, and whatever he is able to accomplish, is only if my Commander allows it. As he mentioned, his master's tricks have not changed since the inception of time, and though he is cunning and crafty in his delivery, we know very well the deeds he will try to deploy next.

Ebenezer: But in your assessment, has he been honest in his responses here today?

MICHAEL: Yes, this deceiver has been honest. A bit overconfident but honest. We are in a battle against one another to control the systems of the world and establish our kingdoms. He and his master have a strong presence in the airwaves at the present moment; however, that is something we are raising up people to take back, men and women whose destinies are catered specifically to those fields.

Ebenezer: I understand. It is good to know that he has been, for the most part, honest during my interrogation. But these men and women that you are raising up—are they immune from the clutches of the prince and his cohorts?

MICHAEL: In this world, in its present form, they are not totally immune. However, the power within them that our Commander has deposited is enough to overcome the wily tricks of my enemy, even if they find themselves exposed to them. They possess the power to be set free, not merely to enjoy themselves, but to do battle and engage in the fight, to overcome in their own lives, and to become channels by which others are set free.

Ebenezer: Michael, I am very much encouraged by this. Very much. You seem to inspire and energize when you speak. I would like to hear more. Your enemy mentioned that the battle you fight is not one of flesh and blood but one of principles, or first truths. So, I assume that you would also agree with this statement, and the key, perhaps, to activating that power is by knowing first truths in a sense? Is that correct?

MICHAEL: That is very much the case. ***The reality you see hinges on foundational moral principles, and therefore, the reality you see has spiritual control.*** One of the first truths, or principles that those under my Commander's allegiance must learn and understand is that my men and I have been assigned to each of them to keep them in all their ways. Just as I have been sent here this evening to answer your petition to my Commander, every person in the kingdom of light has at least two such helpers working day and night to keep them from harm.

Ebenezer: I really like that principle, or first truth, as you call it. You all must be a very busy group then. Are you assigned to protect me?

MICHAEL: Yes! Those who understand who my Commander is and who we are and what we do and believe we can be appropriated at any time very much love this principle. It is a great benefit in the kingdom of the light. Our Commander made it clear to all those given free will that the principle of petition is available to anyone in His kingdom who calls for it. I, however, am not directly assigned to protect you. There was a standoff to prevent this meeting from occurring after your request was made on the 10th of December, and I had to intercede and bring him here myself.

Ebenezer: Standoff? Wow. Well, thank you. I wasn't so sure that anything had happened during any of those sleepless nights, but I am happy to know that there was much going on in another realm that I could not see. You mentioned that your enemy has no power over those with free will unless your Commander allows it. Can you explain that a bit more?

MICHAEL: The prince, through his master, still has access to the throne of my Commander. He must seek His permission before he does anything to those the Commander claims because of me and my men standing guard at all times. My enemy and his legions of demons both need my Commander's permission.

Ebenezer: That is very interesting. So, everything that he is getting ready to do, to unleash rather, into the world is being allowed by your Commander?

MICHAEL: That is precisely accurate. Despite what he has said so boldly today and the confidence with which he has spoken, neither he nor his master is on equal level with my Leader. My Commander has several divine attributes that he simply does not and will not have. He is omnipotent, omniscient, and omnipresent; of those characteristics, his master carries none.

Ebenezer: I am glad you have said this and made it abundantly clear. It is encouraging to know that the two are truly not on an even playing field. But I must ask, and please excuse my ignorance on this matter, but if your Commander is infinitely more powerful than His adversary, then why is he being allowed to run terror on the people of this world and to do his evil deeds in manipulating them in confusion by using distorted principles?

MICHAEL: Great question. Great question, indeed. To answer this question, we must begin at the very beginning. First of all, in the beginning, the quality of everything that our Commander created was good, but something went wrong. Good became bad. The accuser was the bearer of the light, or the knowledge and truth of God, at one time. It was, again, at one time, a beautiful thing. Before he became the accuser, he was the most vibrant of the angels. But he said in his heart, "I will ascend to heaven, and I will raise my throne above the stars of God." Is that not what your master said, Mr. Prince?

(Silence)

PRINCE: Yes. That is what he said. You know this, Michael.

MICHAEL: But wickedness was then found in him. And he was no longer the model of perfection, and his purity left him. His heart became proud, and his wisdom became corrupted and perverted. Do I speak the truth, Mr. Prince?

PRINCE: I cannot speak for my master, but yes, that is the truth, I suppose.

MICHAEL: Mr. Ebenezer, the accuser decided to leave the truth, even though our Commander called him the model of perfection. He lived in the presence of our Great Leader. He lived each moment next to Him, as a cherub in His presence. But his own pride and vanity caused him to be cast down. So, this being set up his kingdom in the air, which he has already somewhat thoroughly explained. This man has only one dream since he was cast down from heaven—he wants to get his fill of worship here on Earth. He has told the absolute truth in that regard. But he needs a body here to make himself legal. So, Ebenezer, in simple terms, this accuser wants to possess you. However, to address your question, the accuser and his followers have only been given freedom for a time. But even in the freedom he has been allotted, he is still carrying out our Commander's purposes, for all the armies of Earth that he may control are still nothing compared to my Commander's power, and He is the One whose glory and majesty will return at the appropriate time.

Ebenezer: It would be great to know exactly when that time will be, as it could perhaps give many people hope—much-needed hope. People have begun to lose hope in this world and in living in general.

MICHAEL: I will tell you this, and I am somewhat sad to say it: the world will see a greater flood of evil in the coming decade that will attempt to destroy all witnesses to my Commander on the face of your Earth. But do not be afraid, for as I have said, even as our adversary is working, we are still working, still protecting, and my Commander will return once more at the appointed time to completely take back the Earth and make right every distorted principle.

Ebenezer: I look forward to this day very much. I hope that it will happen in my lifetime. But please, Michael, tell me: How can one be one of the few whose true allegiance remains with your Commander? In other words, in what areas must he focus his efforts to ensure he remains a tool and instrument of the kingdom of light?

MICHAEL: Ebenezer, may I be so bold as to say that I believe you very well know the answer to the question you are asking.

(Silence)

Ebenezer: I do?

MICHAEL: Yes, you do. For this was the sole purpose for this interrogation or interview today, whichever you choose to call it. Yes, the enemy is at work getting ready to unleash his evil deeds on the entire Earth, spreading fear throughout the hearts and minds of those unaware of his tactics and in those who have become slaves to his principles. But my Commander has brought him here so you can prepare yourself and warn others to prepare, also, for what he will be unleashing. ***Remember, the reality you see hinges on moral foundations, and therefore, the reality you see has spiritual control.*** Now, to recapture what has been said here, what battle is being fought between my Commander and his adversary?

Ebenezer: The battle... hmm. I suppose I may be a bit slow this evening, for it is a bit late, or early, I should say. Forgive me. But I believe what was discussed here is that the battle is not one waged by human hands but is about first truths or principles that have become a part of one's inner man. And yes—***all reality hinges on moral foundations, and therefore, has spiritual control.***

MICHAEL: Yes, you have it exactly right. Please listen to this recording again and again in the coming days because it is of critical importance. In terms of the principles that you and others seeking allegiance to our Commander should adhere to, a critical reason for our discussion today, there are seven that I would encourage you to walk in as you go about your daily life on Earth. In doing so, you can live a life here and now on your Earth that mirrors that of my home country, my Commander's headquarters.

Ebenezer: Live a life here on Earth just as it is in the Heavenlies. Outstanding. I would love to know these principles. As you say, these principles will allow me to be productive in this world, even throughout the next decade? And prevent me from being influenced by the principles of your adversary?

MICHAEL: Yes, that is the truth. The key, once I give you these principles, is to guard them against the systems of Earth over which my adversary wields a great deal of control at the current moment. These will get you through the season of crisis in the coming decade and beyond. I have said it several times, and I will say it again as it is of critical importance: ***The reality you see hinges on moral foundations, and therefore, has spiritual control.***

Ebenezer: And once again, I hear you, and I agree. Very well. I am eager to hear what you have to say. Open up.

MICHAEL: The first principle that one must live by and mark on one's mind and heart in order to make it through the coming decade is the ***principle of purpose***. I am amazed by how many of you humans reject even the idea of death because you know you have not finished what you have been born to start. Death never threatens an Earth Dweller who has discovered his purpose.

Ebenezer: That is a very strong assertion. If I am hearing you correctly, the logical conclusion to your statement is that human beings can die and should die willfully, without the pressure of any external influence?

MICHAEL: That is exactly what I am saying, and the man who understands this can gain the power to defeat even death, something my adversary here finds absolutely repulsive. Purpose gives every man clear confidence about his life and his death. There are so many people who are lost and frustrated, even those that follow my Commander. Have you ever seen a manufacturer who began to build something, and because it didn't become what he intended, he made it into something else? You don't see that. The builder doesn't stop until he gets what he purposed in his mind. The purpose for the product cannot be substituted. ***If you are trying to become something you are not, you are abusing what you are.*** There is no satisfaction besides purpose. Purpose will haunt you. No matter what you plan, if it isn't my Commander's purpose for you, it will not prevail.

Ebenezer: What percentage of people do you know that are living their purpose? Seventy? Eighty?

MICHAEL: Seventy or eighty? Oh no! How about five or ten. If that. There is an enormous amount of squandered potential, a lot of misdirected minds, and many unhappy people. Your world is full of them. Just imagine the positive impact these people could make on your planet if they started doing something they truly valued! Plus, it makes our jobs easier. I can't begin to tell you how miserable it is to have my guys assigned to help people who are doing nothing, always grumpy, and always complaining.

Ebenezer: So, I assume that making money and earning a living are not at all related to living a complete life?

MICHAEL: What?

Ebenezer: So, I assume that making money and ea—

MICHAEL: Yes, I heard you. My response to your question is more related to my total state of shock and disbelief than my inability to hear you. Since I assume you are serious, the answer is no, absolutely no. Money does not, in any way, equate to living a complete life. Foolish is the Earth Dweller who bases his value on money, or any external, physical thing, for that matter…

(Pause)

MICHAEL: Like the human body, which, I should add, is a value that has come to possess many of you, causing many of your younger Earth Dwellers to do once unconscionable things—for the sole sake of making money.

Ebenezer: Hmm...

MICHAEL: Perhaps it has now become clearer why the acceptance of distorted principles can be so damaging and toxic to the human psyche.

Ebenezer: But Michael, I see many of the people I know working jobs I believe they truly enjoy. They walk around the offices smiling and laughing, and they take wonderful vacations with the many bonuses and large commission checks they receive. And the pictures… oh, how they take fabulous pictures and share so the world can see!

MICHAEL: So?! If only you could see what I see!

Ebenezer: Perhaps you could explain. What more is it you see?

MICHAEL: Your Earth is full of people whom everyone believes are doing well, but when they close the door in the evening and turn off the lights, it's hell in the bed. I see them crying, and I see them weeping; I see many angry, frustrated, and disappointed because they know they're not fulfilled. But when they're back in the lights, you Earth Dwellers give them resounding applause. In secret, however, they are as depressed as they can be. Corporate executives, politicians, doctors, bankers, managers, models, many earthlings are doing great things by the standards of others, but yet, they long to do other things. They are, quite simply, out of position. Deep inside, they really want to write. Deep down, they really want to speak. Deep within, they really want to practice law or medicine. Deep within them, they really want to do photography or cater events or cook. Their lack of fulfillment in their gifts will make them frustrated. They are impressing other people yet are depressed and frustrated themselves. My Commander's deep calling and purpose will make them sick if they don't pursue it. The scream of purpose is the loudest one that can ever be heard.

Ebenezer: So, there is a difference for each man between his work and his job. It seems as if his work is what he was born to do, but his job is what the world pays him to do. At least, that is how I see it.

MICHAEL: You see it very well. You see it correctly. Until a man finds his purpose and maps out his destiny, then all he has is a job.

And if all you have is a job, then you really have no reason for getting up in the morning. I don't care how much coffee you drink or how many pills you humans scarf down; if all you have is a job, then you'll lack the energy for living.

Ebenezer: So, purpose and destiny can give energy or take energy, depending on if you have it or if you don't.

MICHAEL: That is exactly right. The man who discovers his true purpose develops a wealth of energy within him that keeps him moving forward. Even against the most impossible odds.

Ebenezer: But tell me, as I am somewhat confused, and my mind is a bit scattered due to the current hour: How does this relate at all to your enemy and avoiding the pitfalls that he aims to deceive us with? Especially in this coming decade?

MICHAEL: It has everything to do with it! Open your eyes! Whenever a man is without a driving purpose, he has no reason to guard his mind from the information he is receiving from the world around him. You heard my adversary's story about the young boy which he took possession of. There is no filter constantly governing his decisions. If a man knows exactly what he should do, then he knows what he shouldn't do. He becomes vigilant in what he allows inside him, outside him, and around him. I have always found it interesting how you humans put so much emphasis on the nourishment you put in your body but fail to guard and protect the nutritional quality of the information that you deposit into your minds. The latter is much more important.

Ebenezer: Can a man or woman be in line with his purpose but be out of line in his principles? In other words, can the influence of your adversary negatively affect the purity of the purpose and vision of the individual?

MICHAEL: I see you are moving two, perhaps three steps ahead. You are as one who has mastered the great game of chess. You speak of both principles and purity, which are both critical for circumventing the enemy's tactics in the coming years. But let's first touch on principles, as they relate specifically to purpose.

(Pause)

MICHAEL: Take, for example, this recorder. This recorder has a purpose in the mind of the manufacturer. The manufacturer built this to fulfill the purpose of recording and transcribing audio for future playback. When the manufacturer desired a product to fulfill the purpose in his mind, he built this so it could fulfill that function. So, he put into it the potential to record and transcribe any and all sounds within a specified radius. So, this recorder inherently has the ability and the potential to record sound. He also inherently built into the purpose and the potential a principle by which this is to operate. So here, in this small recorder, we have a wealth of power and purpose, but we also need to obey the principles by which and under which it is supposed to operate. If those principles instituted by the manufacturer are violated or disregarded for how to operate this recorder, for whatever reason, then its potential and purpose become a curse, and it will not be fulfilled. One of the principles of this product is that it must operate on two AA batteries. In other words, it must be submitted to the principle of power and electricity. Another of the principles for this recorder is that the volume must not be set too high, or else the audio recording will spike and become distorted. A third principle is that this recorder cannot and should not be operated in or underwater. So, this recorder, as you see it here, is a very simple example of how both purpose and potential interact in relation to one another. No matter who you are, what you can do, or where you are from, you will not be successful without adherence, submission, and obedience to principles.

Ebenezer: Both you and your adversary have spoken of the importance of such principles, which leads me to believe with absolute certainty that they must not be avoided or cast aside if one is to win the battle in the coming decade. You speak of a recorder; however, it would be very beneficial if you could also use a human example so that I can better relate.

MICHAEL: Gravity. That is about as simple as a principle gets. If you jump off a ledge, even if you yell and scream for either my men or me to catch you, you will experience the effects of the law you have just violated. You will fall, and depending on how far you are falling, you may die, as you have violated a principle by your own choosing. Neither my Commander nor I ever even get involved because the law has already been given. But take the principle of the body as another example. Your body is not your own. Your body is to be treated as a vessel in which the spirit of my Commander dwells. If you fill your vessel with things that limit this potential, you are violating that principle, and you will face the consequences of that action. I have seen many men violate this principle and wonder why they can no longer accomplish their purpose. Then they ask my Commander for help, wanting Him to bail them out of situations where they have continued to violate His law foolishly. ***They forget that all reality hinges on moral foundations, and therefore, all reality has spiritual control.***

Ebenezer: That is a tough pill to swallow, Michael, but I must readily admit it makes complete sense. Each man must be responsible, then, for learning and adhering to principles. You mentioned that if I were to jump from a ledge, because I have violated the principle of gravity, I would face the consequences for my actions. However, even if you were to attempt to save me, it doesn't appear that you have any wings to do so. Where are your wings?

MICHAEL: You shouldn't believe everything you hear! The idea that angels have wings is about as silly a fictitious story I have ever heard. We angels don't have wings; we are spiritual beings who intervene in human affairs, not superhero characters that you encounter in your movies. Many of the times we encounter people, we appear as men. Why would we need wings? I like driving cars.

Ebenezer: You raise a good point. Perhaps we may need to rethink how we view you and your men.

MICHAEL: That may not be such a bad idea. If you ask me, I look better without wings, anyway. Would you answer the door if the man standing behind it had a large set of feather-like wings?

Ebenezer: Again, you raise another great point. My perception of you has changed. Perhaps there are many angels like you walking among us that we Earth Dwellers cannot see.

MICHAEL: Good. And yes, you, Ebenezer, have seen quite a few of us in your lifetime. Several have even been in your home.

Ebenezer: Really? I don't recall any of these encounters.

MICHAEL: Yes, I know this to be fact. Any time one of us is sent to you or any other Earth Dweller, we must report back to the head office on everything that we encountered here on Earth. If the person we are visiting suspects that we are, in fact, a part of the heavenly forces, we make note of it, for it means that this individual is spiritually attuned and perceptive.

Ebenezer: I see.

MICHAEL: So perhaps, instead of picturing a large flock of angels fluttering through the sky with their magnificent, gigantic wings, it would be wiser and more practical to see an amalgam of differently complected men who reflect, in many ways, the commonality of Earth and the glory of the Heavenlies, my home country.

Ebenezer: Well said. Let's pivot and shift gears. How powerful are you and your comrades?

MICHAEL: Thank you. We angels are POWERFUL. We are created beings, and we are sustained by our Chief. Our power is delegated, and boy, it is awesome, I must say. We have been called the might of our Commander. Just one of us is able to take out your entire city, or any other city, for that matter. We did it before, and we can do it again. Think about it. It took just one of us to roll a stone that it took 15 men to move. Just one of us killed hundreds of thousands of Pharaohs' people overnight. Just one of us. Just one of us put to death 85,000 men in an Assyrian camp. ***Eighty-five thousand.*** I know you are familiar with those stories.

Ebenezer: Yes, I very much am. That *is* some potent force. On second thought, yes, you do appear to be a powerful group. Let us get back, however, to the discussion of the next decade and the practical steps needed to assure one remains immune from the influence of your adversary. I would like to learn more about these principles you speak of.

Chapter 6

The Heavenlies

—

December 31, 2019

As Mr. Bigsby walked with Netzach down the majestic streets of the Heavenlies, he noticed several angels carrying a set of tubes from a building and loading them onto some sort of a conveyor belt mechanism. They loaded thousands and thousands of tubes into a gigantic basket sitting on a conveyor belt that was being manned by several other seraphim. Inside the tubes, Mr. Bigsby noticed a substance, and each of the tubes had a label with a long stream combination of numbers and letters. Netzach, as if to have read Mr. Bigsby's mind, began to explain what he was seeing.

"Those seraphim you see over there," he said, pointing, "work in the lab within that building, the P & P Building, and each one of those tubes you see is filled with a unique set of coding that will be administered to every new Earth Dweller getting ready to be put into motion on the Earth. The Boss has each of these codes locked up deep within Him, and at the appropriate time, He sends word to these seraphim to string certain combinations of characteristics, plans, and purposes and to mix them into these test tubes. Once mixed, they are administered to each Earth Dweller at the point of conception. It's an invisible, almost imperceptible process, but it happens."

Netzach moved toward two of the seraphim standing outside the building who were loading up the basket. He greeted one of them as he plucked one of the tubes from the moving belt.

"You see? This one reads "ABM+E-G." A rather shorter combination, I must say, but one, nonetheless." Netzach handed over the tube to Mr. Bigsby, who at once began to look it over.

"I don't understand. What do the letters mean?" he asked.

"Every combination is different. This particular one means that the Earth Dweller will be given a knack for athletics, business, media, and entertainment, and he will have the capacity to do it on a global scale."

"Interesting," Mr. Bigsby responded. "So, every human being comes to Earth with such a code?"

"Yes, but you can't see it. It's deep within what you Earth Dwellers call the DNA, or makeup, of the individual, and it's really just a piece of the direct image of my Commander. So, in essence, each

Earth-dwelling spirit being in a dirt body has a piece of my Boss's coding within them. It's a very complicated thing, but I hope that makes sense," he added.

Mr. Bigsby nodded. "It does."

Right at that second, two powerful angels zipped right by them as if they had somewhere important to be. The gust of wind that followed caused the plants in the ground near them to bend so far forward that they nearly touched the ground. There was so much activity in the Heavenlies that even Netzach seemed to be getting spun around. He quickly placed the test tube back on the moving conveyor belt and turned his attention toward the path the two giant seraphim were on.

"Those two guys," Netzach began, "are responsible for many of the bigger events you Earth Dwellers have experienced on Earth. Perhaps I'll tell you about them sometime. Just know that when the Boss puts them to work down there, they ***work and get things done.***" Before the angels stormed out of sight, Mr. Bigsby was able to read the backs of each seraph. On one was the word "Goodness" and on the other "Mercy," both written in big, bold letters.

Mr. Bigsby nodded his head as he watched the two monstrous seraphim storm by, disappearing somewhere off into the distance. Despite the fact that Netzach was speaking, half of his mind was focused on other things, for at the moment he had entered the Heavenlies, he had begun to experience something very different. It was as if his emotional state had been altered. He wasn't afraid, and he felt like he was right at home as he moved through the golden streets. Everywhere in the Heavenlies seemed so bright—yet, even with all its beauty and effervescence, it wasn't so much what he saw as what he experienced. Everything just seemed so right, and nothing at all seemed wrong. The sidewalks, the temperature, the shrubs, the infrastructure—it all made him ***feel*** like he was finally home. ***It's beyond peace, more like a deep and abiding peace***, he thought. Everything he saw, all the things he perceived, were alive—there was no sign of death. Even more, all things to him seemed intelligent, as if they could both move and think. ***There is nothing like this on the face of the Earth.***

"Netzach, is everywhere like this?" he asked.

"Like what?" the seraph replied.

"Like this. I feel an overwhelming combination of aliveness and peace."

"Oh. Yes, I suppose. Whatever you're feeling, yes, it's always like this."

Mr. Bigsby nodded as he continued moving along. "I spent my whole life searching for this feeling…" he whispered to himself.

Hearing him, Netzach took a few steps, stopped, and turned to Mr. Bigsby.

"What you're experiencing is the love the Boss has for you. Here, you'll feel like the Commander loves you and only you—no one else." After saying this, Netzach turned his attention north, where a bright, beaming light could be seen way off into the distance, perched atop a hill. The seraph bowed his head for a moment as if listening to a whisper, and then after a few seconds, bowed even more, as if he were acknowledging that he heard a set of instructions. At once, he began moving along, Mr. Bigsby following right behind him.

"Where are we going?" he asked.

"The Boss just sent some information. He wants me to take you to the Windows of Heaven before heading off to see Him," he replied.

It doesn't matter where I go, Mr. Bigsby thought to himself, if everywhere makes me feel as good as I did from the moment the bright lights of the Heavenlies hit me, and I walked through the big, pearly gates.

In that moment, he couldn't imagine being anywhere else.

Chapter 7

Earth

—

December 31, 2019

MICHAEL: So far, we have touched on both purpose and principles as they relate to fulfilling that purpose. The next principle is that of petition.

Ebenezer: Petition?

MICHAEL: Yes, petition. I mentioned it in passing earlier. The first thing you must remember about the principle of petition is that you are dealing directly with my Commander up in the Head Office. My Commander, by His own choice, does nothing on your Earth except that which is allowed by those with a spirit within a physical body. By His own law, the only one that can cast judgment on this Earth is one like you, who has both a spirit and a body. Petitioning is an Earth Dweller representing my Commander's rights on Earth. Petition is necessary because His influence cannot come to Earth without it.

Ebenezer: Hmm. Petitioning. This sounds like something that would occur in the court of law.

MICHAEL: You've got it. That's exactly what it is. Whatever you decide should happen on Earth, the Heavenly Office will allow; likewise, whatever you decide will not happen on Earth, the Heavenly Office will ***not*** allow. Make sense? My Commander does not invade Earth; He is only invited in. And you must give His government the invitation, just as you must give me and my battalion of men instruction.

Ebenezer: That seems too good to be true and too limiting to be true, all at the same time. Whatever I ask the Heavenly Office to do, it will do?

MICHAEL: Yes and no. The question you must ask yourself is this: Does my petition align with His law and His principles that He intends to govern the Earth? If your principles align with those of my adversary, then your law is out of harmony with my Commander's law, and your petition will not be answered. My Commander only answers His word, because His word has already been established as law. One thing you must understand about me and my battalion of angels is that we heed the voice of our Commander's word. When we hear His word, whether that be from you or the Earth Dweller down the street, we send dispatch and attend to it immediately.

Ebenezer: Immediately… I like the sound of that word. How quick is your response time since you have now clarified the fact that you do not have wings?

MICHAEL: Well, we aim for immediate response time once the petition has been processed and vetted by the Head Office. From there, it is communicated to the angels assigned to wait on the individual, and they then take the request from there.

Ebenezer: I find this very interesting, Michael. The request I made to the Head Office, as you speak of, seemed to have taken quite a bit longer than that. Am I wrong?

MICHAEL: Very wrong. We actually responded to your request immediately after the initial processing. As I mentioned to you before, there was a holdup by my adversary's men in that they would not allow for the prince's presence here initially. That is why I had to step in, handle some business, and bring him here myself.

Ebenezer: It sounds like physical force, then, was used to bring about the answer to my petition.

MICHAEL: I won't go into detail on that. Just know that I, myself, have never engaged in combat and come out on the losing end. Though it may take some time, my job is to carry out my Commander's…

PRINCE: Ha! No, no, no. I'll tell you why it took so long. My Adversary simply grew tired of hearing your little measly appeals and wholeheartedly questioned whether a response to your invocation was even necessary. Why answer some little, scanty Earth Dweller who ignored Him for so long in his younger years? How many days did you go without a single word to Him? Guilty, guilty, guilty you are! There. Now you have the truth.

MICHAEL: Mr. Prince, did anyone ask for your opinion? You and I both know that what you've just stated is a bitter and detestable lie. Ebenezer, my Commander is ***always*** eager to hear from you, even if it ***has*** been a while.

Ebenezer: Well, I hope so. That is encouraging. Thank you. But I must ask, if everyone is assigned their own protectors, then how many have been assigned to me? To heed and act upon the words I speak that are directly in line with your Commander's?

MICHAEL: I will show you. Come and see.

(Seats Shifting)

(Inaudibles)

(Door Opens)

…

…

…

…

…

(Door Closes)

(Seats Shifting)

Ebenezer: Wow. Those four big guys are waiting on ***me***?

MICHAEL: Yes, those four, but you saw the two standing and the two sitting in the street, right?

Ebenezer: Yes, there were two patrolling on the driveway, and one was seated on the curb while the other was stationed atop the vehicle. Are they permitted to do that while on duty?

MICHAEL: Of course they are—if they don't have anything to do!

Ebenezer: Well, why don't they have anything to do?

MICHAEL: Because ***you*** haven't given them anything to do. Remember, they are attending to the Commander's word coming from your voice.

Ebenezer: Remarkable. I think many people would benefit if they had such enlightenment or if they could simply see what I just saw. Perhaps it might provide some with a greater sense of peace.

MICHAEL: You raise a very honest point in your assessment. One that adequately leads to the next principle—that of ***persistence***. Do you know how persistence will act as one of the major principles to help you and many others thrive through the coming decade?

Ebenezer: Yes, as a matter of fact, I do. I am very familiar with persistence. When I made my petition to your Head Office, I continued to make it as an act of persistence until I became weary. I knew that if I were to do that, your Commander would hear and would eventually answer me.

MICHAEL: (Laughter)

Ebenezer: That *is* persistence; am I right?

PRINCE: Yes! You are absolutely right!

MICHAEL: No, you are absolutely ***wrong***. And I am glad we are having this discussion. Remember what I tell you now, as many people misunderstand petition and how it relates to persistence. Whenever a request is received at the Head Office, I told you that it would be received if it echoes the words that my Commander has already set forth into law. Correct?

Ebenezer: Correct.

MICHAEL: Now, once that request is received and processed and it is assigned to the appropriate angel, then there are occasions where the delivery of the request may take some time. Remember, the word that my Commander has spoken is pure, undiluted, and as powerful today as it was yesterday or at any other point in history. But your belief, when you petition, must be such that it is in line with what you are petitioning for. This is the next step in the process of petitioning: The angel assigned to deliver that request must ensure that the belief of the individual is not wavering counter to the request. There are certain hindrances to petitioning that each angel must ensure are absent. These hindrances include the hindrance of ***wishful thinking***, the hindrance of ***mental assent***, the hindrance of ***fear***, the hindrance of ***inferiority***, and the hindrance of ***motives***. Each of these hindrances is a product of my adversary, and they are the reasons for which a petition approved in the Head Office remains unanswered.

Ebenezer: I know many people who are waiting on answers to their fervent petitions. Please speak on each one in greater detail so I might know the truth and pass it along to others as well.

MICHAEL: That is precisely what I would like for you to do and one of the primary reasons for this meeting. I can't tell you how frustrating it is to see people who really need help having their petitions put on hold due to the fact that they are operating under such hindrances. So, by all means, please pass this information along. Let's begin with the hindrance of wishful thinking. The hindrance of wishful thinking is a petition not based on a conviction, but one based on doubt and uncertainty. I am sure you have heard many humans say things like, "I hope this happens," or "I hope that works." These people are bound by the hindrance of wishful thinking, and their petitions will be put on hold. Do you follow?

Ebenezer: Yes, I follow. Please proceed.

MICHAEL: The second hindrance is that of mental assent. This hindrance involves petitions made by those who intellectually accept my Commander's law but have not allowed that law to move from mental assent to action. When this person encounters sensory information that radically opposes the answer to his petition, it becomes an obstacle; he is unable to see beyond what his senses tell him.

(Pause)

MICHAEL: Still following?

Ebenezer: Still tracking.

MICHAEL: Perfect. The third hindrance is that of fear. The hindrance of fear is very simple—it is believing what my adversary is telling you through your thoughts, other people, and various mediums more than what my Commander has already established through His law. Your past mistakes should not be a hindrance to your petition, but for many people, they are.

Ebenezer: My past has no bearing on whether my petition is answered or not?

MICHAEL: It shouldn't, as long as you are correctly aligned with His government and not my adversary's. This is a critical point to remember.

Ebenezer: Noted. And the fourth hindrance?

MICHAEL: I feel the need to say that again. Remember, your past should have no bearing on whether your petition is answered or not, as long as you are correctly aligned with His government and not my adversary's.

Ebenezer: Doubly noted.

MICHAEL: Very well. Now the fourth hindrance is that of inferiority. I have seen this do a great deal of damage to even the most capable of people. Feelings of shame and low self-worth can prevent your petitions from being answered. Remember that my adversary uses this as a weapon to hold you Earth Dwellers back from your ultimate release from the grasp of his fingers. If you hate yourself or you lack respect for who you are, then it's a sure sign that you don't even believe you deserve an answer!

Ebenezer: So, self-respect and self-love are both of paramount importance. You are really laying it out plainly for me here. I find it interesting how both the third and fourth hindrances are corollaries—similar in nature.

MICHAEL: I hope so! And yes, one must be kind to and care for himself. It is true that you Earthlings were created in the image of my Commander, and therefore, the mistreatment of yourself is actually the mistreatment of the apex of His creation. The apple of His eye...

Ebenezer: The icing on His cake... the sauce on His spaghetti... the ketchup on His chips... the paint on His brush...

(Silence)

Ebenezer: The peach within His reach...

MICHAEL: (Laughs) Yes. All of those... you've caught the idea.

PRINCE: The itch on His back that can never be scratched...

Ebenezer: Nice try, Mr. Prince. But yes, I have heard this before, Michael, and we each have been endowed by your Commander with certain rights that cannot be taken, or even given, by any man.

MICHAEL: That is correct. Let us move to the last, but certainly not the least, hindrance. That is the hindrance of motives. We have discussed this at some length already; however, I will reiterate once again that it is not your selfish motives or your personal ambitions that move my men and me to act on your behalf, but my Commander's word. Your heart must be positioned so that this is true in action and not merely reflected in your words... which brings me back to the overarching principle of persistence. This is simply describing the process of internalizing the Commander's laws so that they become a part of your inner mind. Getting something into your inner mind takes a dedicated persistence. As you have heard from my adversary, he is also at work, being persistent as well in his attempt to thwart any attempt at my Boss's law entering your inner mind. If he fails in his attempts, your hindrances will be lifted, and your petitions will be carried out swiftly. True persistence is guarding all areas of your life—your friendships, acquaintances, what you look at, and what you hear, so that only what should be deposited into your inner mind is, in fact, deposited. Without this constant persistence, the conviction needed to bring about the answer to your request cannot be birthed.

PRINCE: May I interject? Thank you. All of this talk about hindrances... Ebenezer, can you really trust this guy? ***Remember, you depend on us, and us only, to give you the truth. The real truth. Anything less is a threat to your freedom.*** And you want freedom, don't you? Besides, look at your past; do you ***really*** think my Adversary will listen to your petitions even if He ***could*** answer them? I came here on my own because I wanted to give you the truth.

Ebenezer: Well, yes, I want freedom. But I don't know how much I can trust you, Mr. Prince. At first, you stated you came at the request of your Adversary, and now you state that you came on your own accord. Do you usually vacillate like this between your statements? Nevertheless, you've both given me a lot of information—information that directly conflicts with each other. I see why you both are at war.

PRINCE: It's clear, isn't it? So, whose information will you accept? Perhaps I can sweeten my end of the deal just a bit more. Remember that car and new house and job you wanted? I could have those to you within a week, next Friday at the latest. All you have to do is accept my principles and ignore what my Adversary has told you. Remember how you've been asking for a wife? I can help with that, too. Just name the type of woman you want, and I will ensure that it happens. It'll be a relationship that will be the envy of all your friends and family. You don't want to be single the rest of your life, do you? Go to the grave all alone? What a shame that would be. To avoid that, all you have to do is listen and obey all of the wonderful principles I tell you.

Ebenezer: Is that all I have to do?

PRINCE: Yes, and ignore my Adversary and ***all*** of His words. Simple, isn't it?

Ebenezer: All of that intrigues me, indeed; however, according to your Adversary, again, you are not to be trusted to even the slightest degree. But regardless, I still have a few more questions... I'd like to hear more about what you have to say, Michael. Please continue on regarding the other remaining principles you mentioned.

MICHAEL: Thank you, Ebenezer. And yes, he is a crafty fellow who cannot and should not be trusted! The next two principles are uniquely intertwined in their own way and cannot be ignored if you are to be effective in outmaneuvering my adversary. They are the principles of power and purity. The principle of power is simply this: Every man or woman, when in proper alignment with my Commander, possesses the potency within him that will enable him to accomplish the purpose for which he was placed on Earth to do. Authentic power depends entirely on the Earth Dweller truly knowing himself and becoming familiar with that potency that resides deep within him. That power within him guides the focus of his life and is the enabler that strengthens him to accomplish what he was created to accomplish in the amount of time he was given to do it. Everything on this Earth is dependent upon something else for it to prosper, function, and succeed. This is the power I refer to as it relates to the enabler within you. This power provides the ability to function in a manner directly in line with your purpose. This power is also a wonderful communicator and will act as the navigational system of your life, alerting you as to when you are off or on course in terms of the direction of your life. It's the best map for living any Earth being can have at his disposal.

Ebenezer: Tantalizing. I believe I have, in fact, heard of this power, though I may not have appropriated it to its full extent. For the sake of our conversation, while I have you here with me, please speak and confirm where this power originates from. This power that resides within us.

MICHAEL: Where does the power for this recorder come from? From the one who manufactured it, of course! Remember, a proper relationship with my Commander is the key.

Ebenezer: That makes logical sense. The one that created the product is also the source of its power. Or perhaps it could direct you to the source of power, correct?

MICHAEL: Correct! Not perhaps, but certainly. All manufacturers designate a source of power for their products as well as how that power can be attained.

Ebenezer: How does one go about attaining this power?

MICHAEL: Alignment, alignment, alignment. The source of dynamite within you is given by my Commander. In all reality, it's actually His very nature that He makes available to you. That is the authentic source of power that has been appropriated to you Earth...

PRINCE: I'm really sorry to interrupt, but, uh, to say my Adversary's power is the only one available is not factual in the least. I have appropriated power as well for all those who request it that will exponentially expand their ability to bring about my purposes in the world. With my power, I can promise you more and more things. The house, the cars, the marriage. All of it, remember.

MICHAEL: I would be very careful in whose power you take hold and possession of, for power, as you know, can either bring about good, or it can catastrophically corrupt one entirely. The provincial immature see the end justifying the means under any circumstance, even as it relates to power. To covet material wealth and other vices at the expense of authentic power is a grave mistake that will cripple and stifle your ability for good and turn you over to this weaselly little devil. Remember, it is only by authentic power that one possesses the ability to create new strategies when met with temporary failure on the road toward accomplishing one's purpose. Have you ever met a man who turns away upon facing defeat after defeat in accomplishing his purpose? It is likely that man has not yet connected to the true power that gives him the ability to overcome even the direst of obstacles. Perhaps this man has connected to some other, illegitimate source of power.

Ebenezer: How many sources of power are there? Thousands? Millions?

MICHAEL: The truth is, there are only two sources of power: the one given by my Commander and the one distributed illegitimately by my adversary! One power is authentic; the other power is not. One power leads to more life; the other leads ultimately to death.

One power helps and uplifts others around you, while the other tears them down. Power can come in many variations but can be narrowed down to these two primary sources.

Ebenezer: I think hardly any people would be thrilled to know that they only have two options for the source of power that will allow them to carry out their plans and achieve their purpose. In our culture, as you may know, we are used to having many choices. It is our way of life. To only have two to choose from is against our fundamental principles.

MICHAEL: Oh yes, I am very aware of this, but this is the truth. Since the beginning of time, there have only been two choices, the two that I have spoken of today. Every man must decide his allegiance to which power he will accept and operate under.

Ebenezer: As I look over the landscape of the world, I am not sure I can differentiate between which power is at work within whom. Is there a surefire, foolproof way of knowing which power is at work within us Earth Dwellers, as you call us?

MICHAEL: Of course there is. Power only expands and furthers principles, allowing for greater impact on a larger scale. Think of power as the fertilizer that allows for more growth and ultimately healthier fruit from the seed in a garden. The fertilizer doesn't change the type of seed; it only allows it to grow in size. Power doesn't change principles; it only allows for the fruit of those principles to be proliferated and furthered to a greater proportion. Good fertilizer can only be applied to good seeds, and bad fertilizer can only be applied to bad seeds. The power given by my Commander will only further expand His principles; my adversary's, his own. If you are aware of what principles underlie those you see throughout your society, you can see which power is at work on either a large or small scale.

Ebenezer: I am not one familiar with fertilizer and its impact on seeds; however, if there are only two sources of power, I guess I long to be on the side of the power in which you possess. For it is through your power that the prince was required to show himself here today, correct?

MICHAEL: That is correct. But there is another aspect to power that you must be aware of also, and it acts as the other side of the same coin. It is the last principle you must give your efforts to, and it acts as the glue that binds everything I have said together. It is the principle of purity. Remember this statement: ***The source of power, or the potency that is within you, can be subverted and pushed down if you fail to recognize and operate under the principle of purity.***

Ebenezer: Even if it is legitimate power, as you have just discussed? If so, I would say that this, by far, *is* the glue that binds all that you've said together. I am eager to hear more.

MICHAEL: As you should be. And yes, even if it is legitimate power. You see, your mind receives information from your senses, and the information from your senses that goes into the mind is deposited into your soul. The soul is made up of your will and your emotions. Your soul then takes that information from your senses and deposits it into your spirit, which is the source of the power that I just discussed with you earlier. Your spirit, your body, and your soul are all interrelated. The soul receives from the spirit and discerns whether what it has received is right or not. This is where the power under which you find yourself influenced becomes of paramount importance. If what you are receiving from your senses is corrupt, meaning the principles are incorrect, then your soul will be damaged, and even if your spirit does not agree, it will be subject to your soul and the information that has been downloaded into it. So, the principle of purity is ensuring that what is received by the soul, body, and spirit are all aligned as one, integrated fully with the intentions of the one in whose allegiance you follow.

Ebenezer: This seems like the technical explanation for the principles you and your adversary have discussed over and over again that you are seeking to gain control over. The principles for which you find yourselves at war.

MICHAEL: Once again, your assessment is correct. From a practical standpoint, your purity depends entirely on what you allow to enter through your senses: what you see, hear, taste, smell, and feel. Eventually, all of that will be deposited into your soul and will cripple even the power of your spirit if it's not integrated into one.

Ebenezer: I'm glad I'm on the right track. How, then, can one walk in complete purity?

MICHAEL: The irony of all of this is that ***you alone*** have the power to decide whether you do so or not. It is on you to decide how much or how little you regulate the information being deposited into your soul. You alone are the one who decides what ultimately will amplify or subvert the spirit within you.

Ebenezer: I see. So, what you are saying is that I have the power to decide the fate of the next decade? Is it really up to me?

MICHAEL: Yes. Precisely. Remember, you and all Earth Dwellers decide what happens on this Earth. ***You decide***, as you have been given the management responsibility over Earth's resources. Whatever you allow, the Head Office will allow. Whatever you don't allow, the Head Office will not allow either. The power is in your hands.

Ebenezer: Then man has incredible choice and incredible power over how he responds to the currents of life. Whether he will succeed or fail, whether he will triumph or fall. It seems there is a unique freedom that is within our grasp that many a man has perhaps not tasted or experienced yet.

MICHAEL: A unique freedom, indeed. There is a misconception of what true purity is and how it is revealed in our lives. True purity, when it comes down to it, is simply the integration of the body, spirit, and the soul into one. When those three align, the person is said to be pure.

Ebenezer: If I understand correctly, then a man can be completely evil and still considered pure?

MICHAEL: If the man's body, spirit, and soul are all evil, then yes, that man is living in purity. That is not to say that the way he is living is correct.

Ebenezer: That seems to be too unbelievable to be true.

MICHAEL: Perhaps. But unlike my adversary here, I aim only to speak the truth. This occurrence is not only unique to purity; it is also a characteristic of the term "character" itself, as you Earth Dwellers know it.

Ebenezer: Answer me this: How does the term "character" fit this definition as well? On what grounds of knowledge do you make this claim?

MICHAEL: By simple definition. My Commander is one, meaning He is completely integrated. In other words, He never changes. A person with ulterior motives is a person without character. So, to have character, or to be one, means you have arrived at a point where you are completely free from any dichotomy. You are only one person, not two. Your greatest battle as an Earth Dweller is between the dichotomy, or two personalities, within you. And it begins with the senses, is filtered through the spirit, and ends with the soul.

Ebenezer: This secret self, does everybody have it?

MICHAEL: I like that term, the secret self. Yes, every Earth Dweller begins this life with a secret self. However, it is a lifelong pursuit to become one, or whole. The more your secret self can become public, the closer you come to becoming pure, or one.

Ebenezer: It appears this is something everyone should strive for. This, too, is difficult in my world as the majority of Earth Dwellers, or people, don't want others to see their "baggage." But I take your word as true. I should ask you this: What are the benefits of becoming "one" beyond what you have described? In a practical sense?

MICHAEL: It's very simple; the foundation of completeness is character. It is as simple as that. If you have no character, you cannot be whole or complete, and you will not be one.

Chapter 8

Earth

—

December 31, 2019

Ebenezer: You know, your statements have me thinking a great deal.

MICHAEL: About?

Ebenezer: Well, the world is full of leaders who have fallen due to failures in character, and it has left us with many problems, in my opinion.

MICHAEL: What type of problems?

Ebenezer: Well, take, for instance, the issues concerning race here in the United States. I'm sorry to bring this up again, as I alluded to this earlier in an indirect question I presented to your adversary. Perhaps you can expound on it a bit more. We seem to be living in a time where such failure in character has led to a lack of moral authority concerning issues like prejudice and racism. At least, that is how I see it.

MICHAEL: You have communicated an interesting analysis. As I watch what is and has been transpiring on your Earth, and as my Commander watches as well, we have no choice but to be concerned. Yes, character plays a role in every earthly conflict. Issues regarding race are no exception. And yes, failure in this arena has led to the degradation of all moral authority on these issues.

Ebenezer: I knew it. And what are your chief concerns?

MICHAEL: The solutions you humans have deployed to solve your problems. And how you have analyzed the problem. And the leadership that is speaking out on the problem and the principles they refer to. Or perhaps I should say the lack thereof.

Ebenezer: I am indeed glad then that I have brought this up for discussion. Over the last several years, or decades rather, men and women have become increasingly more impatient with those who show any form of discrimination toward others. But I suppose I am surprised by your comment that we somehow lack solutions. Wherever I turn, I see people striving and working tooth and nail to bring about change for those experiencing the effects of living in such a society.

MICHAEL: Tell me, as I am curious to know, what solutions do you see?

Ebenezer: Reform. In the form of policy changes in the various systems, but primarily in law enforcement, housing, education…

MICHAEL: Systemic reform is good; however, I would challenge you to consider other possibilities in light of what has been discussed today. Especially given the fact that you have been doing battle over the same issues for quite some time within your Earth. Specifically, think about what we have discussed concerning power. Remember, the potency of my Commander will only further expand His principles; my adversary's, his own. What principles underlie racism within a society? Are they not those of my adversary?

Ebenezer: Yes, I would agree with that statement.

MICHAEL: But what about the solution? Is the solution in line with my Commander or my adversary?

Ebenezer: I consider that a silly question. The solutions are all in line with your Commander's.

MICHAEL: That is incorrect. The dominating solutions you humans have deployed are not in line with my Commander's ***for this time and in this season.***

Ebenezer: For this time and in ***this*** season? I suppose I'm back to playing checkers, Michael. Please explain further.

MICHAEL: The key to understanding the usefulness of authentic power is understanding that it gives one the ability to be able to accomplish his or her purpose. I stated this earlier. My Commander provides the fullness of Himself and His nature and deposits it into each available Earth Dweller, and it then acts as a co-partner to bring about the purposes for which that human was created. This is critical because circumstances could call for a change in strategy based on the time and the season. It appears you humans are deploying strategies that were applicable to your previous generations but not for the current generation or season in which you find yourselves living now. Don't get me wrong; at one point, they were good strategies. So, perhaps I should explain a bit further... you humans have categorized three important periods in your nation's history. The first you call the American Revolution, which established your nation as free and governed by a system you call democracy. The second is the Civil War, which you fought to eradicate the institution of slavery. The third was the American Civil Rights movement, which was conducted to change human behavior related to segregation and discrimination practices. That was a period of intense policy change...

Ebenezer: And the policy change must continue.

MICHAEL: Policy change is important; however, is it necessary for the Earth Dwellers among you to rise and speak directly to the real problem?

Ebenezer: If you are again suggesting that human beings are somewhat off base in how they currently address these issues, I am still not following.

MICHAEL: That is precisely what I am suggesting.

Ebenezer: Okay, make it plain. What is the real problem, then?

MICHAEL: The real problem is that your fellow men have failed to take total responsibility for the policies ruling their own ***hearts***. I am not speaking of outward responsibility, but inward. One must first embody justice before it can completely be given or bestowed on others. That underlying problem cannot be changed through legislation alone; it can only be eradicated through a deeper transformation of the heart, or the inner mind. A man can be set free physically but still not be accepted as an equal if his former oppressor's heart has not changed. A man can be set free physically, and even be accepted by his former oppressor, but still live with the residual effects of his former oppression if his heart, or inner mind, remains unchanged, and he continues to see himself in the light of his former oppression. Oppression of any kind affects both the oppressor and the oppressed. Therefore, I will lay it to you plainly: There is a stain on the heart of you Earth Dwellers, from the least of you to the greatest, from the smallest to the biggest, from the richest to the poorest, from the blackest to the whitest, that must be eradicated through a transformation of the inner mind, or the heart. ***Remember, the reality you see hinges on moral principles, and therefore, the reality you see has spiritual control.*** That is the beginning of true justice, as my Commander sees it.

Ebenezer: And how does one do that? Specifically?

MICHAEL: Through a transformation of the inner mind. However, as I have said, without true authentic power, one is left without the strategies to overcome the problems you Earth Dwellers are experiencing in your time. Problems that stem forth from the heart or inner mind. This power, I know as a fact, is so useful to you Earthlings because it will assist you in this transformation. I will not tell you what specific strategies to deploy; you must connect to this power yourself, submit to it, and discover it relentlessly. I would also advise you to look through this recording carefully upon completion of this discussion, as you may find a few clues that will guide you further toward a solution based upon the things my adversary and I have stated.

Ebenezer: Very well. So, to reiterate, the key to the problems we Earth Dwellers face is a change in heart or a true mental transformation?

MICHAEL: Based on knowledge of the truth and a revelation of the strategies that my Commander has made available through the power He has deposited in those ready and wanting to receive it.

Ebenezer: I must say, my mind is turning like a propeller at the moment. I would like to dig deeper into this topic while I still have the chance. Because, in all honesty, I am a bit confused as to what I can say to the world, to my peers that has not already been said. I now know I must connect to this power and appropriate it as my co-partner to bring about the strategies for change within my society; I have noted that. However, I would very much enjoy hearing from you how you assess the various incidences of violence that have been inflicted upon seemingly helpless individuals at the hands of others. Incidences that have even been captured and disseminated by innocent bystanders. Based on your statement earlier, man is the responsible agent on this Earth, and he must take responsibility for this issue and for dealing with it effectively. Is that correct?

MICHAEL: Yes, you Earth Dwellers are the responsible ones. I can offer my assessment of the situation. For one, the fact that you Earthlings have reacted to these incidences, whether the reaction is in line with my Commander's principles or not, means there is hope. For the conscience of you humans have not been fully stained. However, it takes careful analysis and self-reflection to really take full inventory of the situation and realize that the issue is not only between the one who is being oppressed and the one administering the oppression.

Ebenezer: Okay, how would you analyze it then? If you were I, in what other ways would you view it?

MICHAEL: Well, other than what you already know about the oppressed and the oppressor, how about the Earth Dwellers who have captured the acts via their recording contraptions and have acted to expose the evil deeds to the world? How about the others who have stood idly by and watched the events transpire? Is there any blood on their hands? My Commander once told a story about a Samaritan who was traveling along a road and saw a man who was not of his kind lying on the path, beaten and robbed. Two other men had passed before him, but they did not stop. Yet this man who was from a completely different background stopped to help and tend to him.

Ebenezer: Yes, I have heard that story.

MICHAEL: Yes, it's a popular one. What you don't realize is that the road in which they were traveling was a very dangerous road and was every bit conducive for ambushing. So, anyone who stopped to help the man would have been putting his ***own*** life at risk. The Samaritan was fulfilling the highest act of love in putting aside his own well-being for a complete stranger. Now, with that said, the individuals who were present during some of these incidences, were they fulfilling the highest act of love by recording the events?

Ebenezer: I know where you're going with this, and I would have to say that although it could be said that they were doing a good thing, that no, they were not. They weren't doing the ***best*** thing.

MICHAEL: Why?

Ebenezer: Because the highest act of love in that situation, as you have stated, would be to have stepped in to ***stop*** the man committing the injustice… even if it cost them their lives.

MICHAEL: Correct. However, as we have said time and time again, if the principles one lives by are incorrect, then the heart, or inner mind, is not correct.

Ebenezer: And what about the others?

MICHAEL: Yes, the others. There were some who neither recorded nor did anything to resolve the issue they were seeing. They simply sat by and took in the experience. I believe that is 99 percent of you Earth Dwellers. Simply consuming but doing nothing.

Ebenezer: I've heard that said before.

MICHAEL: The consumer mentality is dangerous and takes one further and further away from true unconditional love. It spirals one down the deep corridors of hopelessness and ever reaches, always wanting despair, into a dark night devoid of even the dimmest of stars. True unconditional love, as my Commander sees it, is laying one's entire life down for anoth...

PRINCE: Ewww. Ugh, someone cue the violin and then call me an ambulance.

Ebenezer: Hush, Mr. Prince. But Michael, what would your Commander have done if He was a bystander while some of these injustices were occurring?

MICHAEL: It is becoming more and more clear that you are in dire need of a hearing aid, my friend.

PRINCE: It's okay! No need to remember anything he says. Only remember the things I have told you. Freedom, remember. Truth, remember.

Ebenezer: Freedom, truth, yes, yes, I know. I have begun to learn that at many times the best answers usually present themselves while in deep silence and contemplation. With that said, there is another topic that I have wondered about for some time in my moments of silence that I would like to get your opinion on, if you would allow it, Michael. It is in regard to charity, or what some humans, or Earth Dwellers as you call us, call philanthropy.

MICHAEL: Ah, charity. You Earth Dwellers adore it.

Ebenezer: I see by the tone of your voice that you may have strong opinions about it, one way or another.

MICHAEL: Let me hold my tongue and hear out your question. Proceed.

Ebenezer: Well, it isn't so much a question as it is an assessment of the overall system, based on what we have discussed thus far concerning true, unconditional love. You see, many humans, or Earth Dwellers, have used their wealth and resources to invest in causes that they care deeply about, causes they would like to see transformed and significantly changed…

MICHAEL: I am aware of this, yes.

Ebenezer: Great. I must be honest; I have struggled with this to some degree because I have always been one to question the motives of those who do give, as it seems that at many times one's giving can become so impersonal that it ultimately becomes ineffective.

MICHAEL: Ebenezer, a man may be self-centered in his self-denial and self-righteous in his self-sacrifice; his generosity may feed his ego, and his piety may feed his pride. To that man, benevolence becomes egotism, and martyrdom becomes spiritual pride.

Ebenezer: Yes... what you just said, I've heard it said before. So, I assume you would agree that the current system of "giving back," as we know it, is ineffective? Or could it be riddled with self-centeredness and pride?

MICHAEL: Let me ask you this: How should you define unconditional love?

Ebenezer: Back again to unconditional love… let's see… unconditional love, or the highest act of love, is an individual choosing to lay his entire life down for another.

MICHAEL: Precisely. But I must now add to that definition with respect to the current topic. True unconditional love is not only one choosing to lay his entire life down for another but doing so with the mentality and heart posture that he is not expecting anything in return. So, with that working definition, how would you evaluate your Earth Dwellers' current system of "giving back"?

Ebenezer: Well, one of the primary vehicles for giving back is through the not-for-profit, which means the organization is not looking to make any money off the donation that was given to it. I don't know the exact definition, but that, in my understanding, is the gist of it.

PRINCE: That sounds like true compassion and unconditional love to me!

MICHAEL: On the surface, yes. But what else?

Ebenezer: What do you mean, what else?

MICHAEL: Are they, or are they not receiving anything in return?

Ebenezer: Well, there are a few benefits that such giving provides. For one, most of these organizations are structured this way, which allows for those that give to receive a charitable deduction against their own income.

MICHAEL: Anything else?

Ebenezer: I'm not sure I can think of anything else...

MICHAEL: You can. What else concerning the system do you know about?

Ebenezer: Well, I know that those receiving donations face limitations as to how involved they can be in influencing such things as legislation or supporting political candidates…

MICHAEL: Interesting.

Ebenezer: Interesting… what?

MICHAEL: I will provide no further opinion on this and will leave that to you to draw out your own conclusion based on the knowledge I have given you and the assessment you have brought to the table.

Ebenezer: Mr. Prince, any thoughts on the matter?

Prince: (Tapping Finger) … Moving on.

Chapter 9

The Heavenlies

—

December 31, 2019

Netzach and Mr. Bigsby continued along the path toward their destination, and Mr. Bigsby continued to take in all of his surroundings. He noticed to his right a large, clear, winding river flowing through the bustling city in the opposite direction, and heavenly beings were using its water for various things. Some were in it, some were scooping it, others were simply watching it—it was a powerful and abundant river, and it was clear that its water was giving each of the heavenly beings their sustenance. Mr. Bigsby tried to follow the river with his eyes all the way to its source but couldn't. He did, however, notice that it spiraled onward and onward, in the exact direction of the beaming light that Netzach had bowed to earlier, a light that appeared to be illuminating every area that the two went. As they walked along the path, Mr. Bigsby also noticed many beautifully built mansions, and all the roads leading toward them were a clear and brightly tinted gold. Even the path they walked on, as he looked down at his feet, appeared to be such—so much so that he could see his own reflection staring directly back at him. Various species of beautiful flowers were planted along the stunning mansions. He noticed tiny signposts out in front of them, each stating the same thing: "Positions of Authority."

"Netzach, do people need to eat in this place?"

Netzach continued along but shook his head "no," all the while reaching from somewhere Mr. Bigsby couldn't see and pulling out a small bag of chips.

"Here in the Heavenlies, there is nothing like hunger or thirst. The Fountain of the Water of Life provides the sustenance every heavenly being needs. There is eating and drinking here, but it isn't for the same purpose as to how you Earth Dwellers use it. Here, eating and drinking are for enjoyment, not for sustenance," he added while taking a tiny bite.

They continued along, passing more beautifully crafted mansions, various heavenly beings, and numerous species of plants. All the while, the winding river beside them kept flowing, still crystal clear. Off to the far right, on the other side of the river, a group of angels congregated together, surrounding something massive, a clock it seemed, whose pendulum was slowly swinging back and forth.

"What is that, Netzach? What are those seraphim doing?" Mr. Bigsby asked.

Without breaking stride or even turning his head to look, Netzach began to wave his arm from left to right.

"What you see is called the Pendulum of Life, and it swings between darkness and light, midnight and morning. Think of it like you would a thermometer. A thermometer reads the temperature of the environment. In the same way, the Pendulum of Life reads the temperature of the Earth and provides us in the Heavenlies with a reading of the amount of darkness that exists in the Earth at any particular time. The pendulum stays stagnant for most of the day, but at the appropriate time, based on the choosing of the Boss, it begins to sway for exactly three minutes and then settles on the current 'temperature' on Earth. Usually, quite a few angels make their way over to watch it swing. I, myself, have other things to do, as we are constantly giving more and more new residents tours of our facilities."

"Interesting," Mr. Bigsby commented as he turned his entire body and began walking backward, watching both the seraphim and the pendulum sway back and forth. ***What a sight to see***, he thought.

After a few moments, the two reached a massive building, unlike anything Mr. Bigsby had seen up until that time, and one that was more beautiful and vibrant and heavily adorned with all types of precious stones. It reached up as high as the eye could see, and it was plastered with large windows on every single side.

Netzach stopped in front of the building and placed his hands on his hips, admiring it. "Jasper, sapphire, and emerald adorn it, to name just a few. Twelve different precious stones are placed right into the fabric of this building you see right here. All of them were created by my Boss, for Himself. Are you ready to go inside?"

Mr. Bigsby, mesmerized over the height and the beauty of the architecture of the building, nodded his head "yes," though he hadn't really paid any attention to the question.

"Come along then. As I mentioned, this building is the WOH building, or what you Earth Dwellers may have referred to as the 'Windows of Heaven.'"

As the two entered, Mr. Bigsby noticed that the place was bustling with various kinds of seraphim, both large and small, who were manning each of the windows that riddled the walls of the building. Next to each of them was what appeared to be a large, black storage box, and thousands upon thousands of them lined the interior walls of the building right next to a corresponding window. Every few seconds, one of the seraphim would bow his head in the same manner Netzach had done and proceed to open up both the window where they were standing and the large storage shed they were manning. It all happened at lighting-like speed, however—so quickly that Mr. Bigsby couldn't tell what was actually leaving the shed storage and exiting through the window.

Mr. Bigsby, paying little attention to the angels at work, continued walking down the long, seemingly endless hallway of angels, windows, and storage sheds, watching them open and close at blistering speed.

"This is just one of about a thousand floors," Netzach mentioned.

"Incredible. What are these storage sheds?" Mr. Bigsby asked.

Netzach stopped at one of the units, greeted the seraph attending it, and carefully opened it up. There were treasures upon treasures of different kinds inside of it.

"Wow," Mr. Bigsby exclaimed.

As fast as he opened it, Netzach quickly shut the unit closed.

"These storage houses belong to every living Earth Dweller. Every Earth Dweller has unique treasures of various kinds within his storage space and has a delegated seraph on duty manning it to give him access to the things inside when appropriate.

Mr. Bigsby acknowledged the statement and turned his attention to the rest of his surroundings. He noticed that some angels were sitting down, while others seemed extremely busy, facilitating and overseeing the opening up and closing of the windows and each respective storehouse. He noticed that some storage houses even looked worn down and overused, while others looked brand-new, and some were even covered with cobwebs.

"Hello, Netzach. How are you?" A seraph was just passing by who appeared to be overseeing each of the seraphim manning the windows.

"Oh, things are splendid, Barachiel. How are you?"

"Things have slowed down quite a bit, but outside of that, I can't complain much," he responded, shrugging his shoulders.

"I hear you. Hopefully, things will pick up soon. Do you have the key to the 1,000th floor?" Netzach asked him.

Barachiel reached into his pocket, pulled from it a single key, and tossed it over to Netzach.

"Here you go. Good luck up there," he remarked.

Both Netzach and Mr. Bigsby continued walking down the long corridor until they reached a side entrance that looked something like an elevator. But instead of pushing any buttons, they were instantly transported upward until they reached another floor. A sign on the wall read "The 1,000th Floor."

As they stepped off, Mr. Bigsby noticed that the seraphim on this floor were all occupied with things other than their assigned storehouse and the window they presumably should have been manning. Netzach paced past a few of the storehouses, inspecting each of them with great diligence until he finally stopped at one in particular, which was overrun with cobwebs. There were no seraphim manning it, and there was a red piece of tape labeled on it that simply read "REASSIGN." He reached for the handle and tried with all his might to open it.

It wouldn't budge.

"Some help here?" he requested, turning to Mr. Bigsby.

Mr. Bigsby walked over and began to use his strength to try and open the storehouse. After some prying, it finally swung open. Inside were the most beautiful treasures Mr. Bigsby had ever seen. It was so full that many of the treasures fell out from inside it.

"Incredible. This person must be important. Whom does this belong to?" he asked.

Netzach went over to the front door of the unit and began picking off the red tape. After a few moments, he waved for Mr. Bigsby to come over. To his surprise, the name plastered across the front of the storehouse was none other than his.

Chapter 10

Earth

—

December 31, 2019

Ebenezer: Okay, moving on then. I would like to ask you both a few questions related to the true meaning of several words as they relate to both of your missions to assess whether there may be any similarities or differences between your fundamental beliefs beyond what we have already discussed here today. Do the two of you agree to participate?

MICHAEL: Yes.

PRINCE: Ask your questions, and if I am in the answering mood and oblige, I may provide my perspective.

Ebenezer: I can't say I wasn't expecting that response from you, Mr. Prince, so I will proceed anyway.

PRINCE: Proceed.

Ebenezer: I would first like to inquire of both of you as to your perspective and opinion on the meaning of the words echoed at the beginning of our Declaration of Independence. As it reads, "We hold these truths to be self-evident, that all men are created equal, that they are endowed by their Creator with certain unalienable rights, that among these are life, freedom, and the pursuit of happiness." Please, Michael, could you first define for me, in your own words, the meaning of the word ***freedom***.

MICHAEL: That is simple. Freedom is responsibility, self-determination, and work.

Ebenezer: Mr. Prince?

PRINCE: Simple indeed! Freedom is defined as a state where one is accountable to no being other than himself, but also a state where he may live in a constant state of dependence on others—a state where he has no obligation to pursue and achieve any type of life-giving work on his own initiative.

MICHAEL: Let me also add that freedom is doing the right thing.

PRINCE: No, true freedom does not define what is right or wrong, for right and wrong are left up to the individual to decide. Right and wrong are relative to each individual, and therefore, to the majority within the context of democracy.

MICHAEL: Freedom means one seeks to control his own behavior without the coercion of external forces such as government.

PRINCE: In true freedom, external coercion and control are necessary to maintain a functioning society!

MICHAEL: Freedom, I should add, is a major attribute of my Commander.

PRINCE: Freedom is a major attribute of mine as well. In fact, my master promises it to all of his followers in abundance, and there is no one to regulate what you say or do!

MICHAEL: Freedom is the power of the mind to choose between alternatives.

PRINCE: Yes, freedom does permit one the right to choose between alternatives, ***but*** with no restraints on those alternatives.

MICHAEL: Freedom is paramount to moral responsibility.

PRINCE: What is moral responsibility? True freedom has no moral responsibility and will never have any moral responsibility.

MICHAEL: Freedom is the right for you Earth Dwellers to govern, manage, and rule your area of gifting to complete your earthly assignment. There is no freedom without law, and therefore, freedom is always under law.

PRINCE: True freedom does not receive its rights from anyone other than oneself. There is no delegation in freedom, as I see it.

True freedom does not require any specific assignment. In true freedom, one is free to use anything in any way he feels he would like to use it and do whatever he would like with all resources he finds available to him, whether the resources belong to him or not. In true freedom, law does not exist, and therefore, one can do and has permission to do what one wants at all times. Could anything be better?

MICHAEL: Ebenezer, true freedom, as I've described it, is the only form of freedom that can genuinely satisfy and uplift the soul.

PRINCE: Hmm… true freedom does not seek to satisfy the soul but the flesh, which, as we all know, provides one with the greatest gratification. Sensual gratification, that is.

…

(Pause)

…

Ebenezer: Is that all? Clearly, you are both at odds.

MICHAEL: That is all that needs to be said regarding true freedom as we both see it. And yes, I could have told you that beforehand.

Ebenezer: Thank you. Let's move on to another term that I have heard used frequently by us humans, or Earth Dwellers as you call us, but I have yet been able to adequately define it or confirm its meaning. By the way, thank you again, Mr. Prince, for responding to these questions, as they were not included on the original list.

PRINCE: Eh.

Ebenezer: Actually, before we get to that four-letter word that I have yet been unable to define, perhaps we could quickly breach the topic of government. Mr. Prince, are you and those who follow you Democrats or Republicans?

PRINCE: Great question. It depends.

Ebenezer: Depends on?

PRINCE: On the policies, of course. Whosever policies more adequately align with freedom as I've described it is the party in which my master's followers and I pledge our allegiance.

Ebenezer: So, if I am understanding correctly, you and your people take your time and evaluate the issues prior to making a decision as to whether you will align yourselves with the Democratic or Republican party?

PRINCE: Yes, that is correct. We aren't necessarily conservative or progressive in our beliefs, for those, again, can change depending on which of you Earth Dwellers is holding office.

Ebenezer: Interesting. I would have thought otherwise...

PRINCE: You undoubtedly thought wrong, my friend. Are we left, or are we right? It simply just depends.

Ebenezer: Interesting indeed... Michael, do you and your Commander take the same position as it relates to politics?

MICHAEL: What?

Ebenezer: Do you and your Commander tak—

MICHAEL: Yes, my friend. I heard you. But why are you asking me such a question?

Ebenezer: Well, I must say that it is quite an important question to ask, especially during this time. Have you not been permitted to speak on such matters by your Commander?

MICHAEL: My friend, Democrat or Republican does not exist in either my vocabulary or in my Commander's. Those words ring as words of treason in the Heavenlies. Therefore, I will not, and cannot in good conscience, utter even one word on such a subject.

Ebenezer: Okay… Well, what can you speak on as it relates to politics?

MICHAEL: You mean government.

Ebenezer: Sure.

MICHAEL: My Commander is the Head of State, and as Sovereign Ruler, His word is His law. There is no vote. There is no debate.

Ebenezer: So… Do you lean more left or more right?

(Silence)

Ebenezer: I guess we'll just move on. Umm… Now, I would like for both of you to describe the word ***love*** as a noun, a verb—however you see it. Mr. Prince, I will allow you the honors…

PRINCE: As you should. And don't mind him; he's always been a bit one-sided when it's come to discussing the satisfying world of politics. Love has as its chief focus the satisfaction of oneself and oneself only. True love carries with it the idea that everything externally has been made available for the pleasure and satisfaction of the individual, regardless of the needs of others.

Ebenezer: Interesting. Michael?

MICHAEL: True, authentic love is simple—it is a radical kindliness for oneself but, at the same time, a radical rejection of oneself in favor of a tenderness toward others.

PRINCE: Does that even make sense? Come on... This isn't a philosophy class!

Ebenezer: Interesting, Michael. Mr. Prince, let him speak. Can you expand on that a bit more? How is it possible to radically love oneself and, at the same time, radically reject oneself in favor of others, as well?

MICHAEL: Sure. To radically love oneself means that one seeks complete alignment with the higher purpose for which he was created. Doing so effectively means the Earth Dweller does everything within his power to develop himself, preserve himself, and take care of himself...

Ebenezer: And to the other half? The radical rejection of oneself?

MICHAEL: A radical rejection of oneself suggests he does it for a different end. He does it not for his own pleasure but for the glory of the One whose resources he is called to steward and for the benefit of those around him so they, too, can experience and live in a world reflecting that glory, making their lives better as a result.

Ebenezer: So essentially, one develops himself as much as possible so that he can then pour himself out to others and for others?

MICHAEL: Yes.

Ebenezer: How else can you describe it?

MICHAEL: In simple terms, when one gives up his life for another, that is the ultimate rejection of self, or a radical kind of love. You asked earlier about some of the tension between you Earth Dwellers in various people groups on your Earth today, and we have touched on how this type of radical love might apply to this situation.

Ebenezer: Yes, we have. However, I am interested in hearing a bit more on it, as to how radical love, as you describe, would look in that particular scenario. I believe you stated that in the case of one individual harming another, with such an incident being captured, you would present that radical love would call for those surrounding to go above and beyond the normal duty of love to a radical kind of love—a love which places a man's own life on the line in the place of their own. Is that correct?

MICHAEL: Yes, that is a radical love, indeed. Many of you, I know, will not agree with this statement. As a matter of fact, I would say not a few people on this Earth would even give it a second thought. What you Earthlings fail to understand is that this, too, is just as much an issue of the heart as the one perpetrating the actual crime. Again, I only say it as I see it. Perhaps there is some work to be done on your part upon completion of this interview.

Ebenezer: Indeed, I can agree that there is some work to be done. I must ask you another question, however. One in which your adversary has already addressed. Your enemy has already discussed his prototype victim—one whom he is able to begin influencing from a very young age, teaching them his principles so that they begin to live them out upon reaching adolescence. He mentioned that the structure of the family is of paramount importance to his goals. On the opposite end of the spectrum, who would you say is your ideal victim, if that can be said of your relationship to those who are consistently acting under your control?

MICHAEL: If by "victim," you refer to those who express their ultimate allegiance to my Commander in both word and deed, then absolutely, the aim is to have every Earth Dweller be "victimized." Let me address this by first speaking on my adversary's dialogue regarding the human will and every man having a choice as to whom he places his ultimate allegiance.

Ebenezer: Yes, I was hoping you would. Is this incorrect?

MICHAEL: Certainly not. It is a very true statement that every Earth Dweller is given a choice as to whom he will place his allegiance. From the moment of birth, the child is placed into a world that is highly unfavorable to building a healthy and fruitful allegiance to my Commander, and therefore, the family is very important, extremely important, during the Earth Dweller's formative years.

Ebenezer: I see how that may be the case. Of this family structure that you speak of, I would like to know more. Within the family, who is most important to its success? Of influencing the children within the family to follow your Commander?

MICHAEL: That is a very serious question; however, I will ask you to rephrase it just a bit before I address it. The better question, I would say, is to ***whom*** within the family has the ultimate responsibility been placed for the growth, protection, and preservation of its structure?

Ebenezer: I oblige… Michael, who in an Earth Dweller's family has been given ultimate responsibility for the preservation of the household?

MICHAEL: I'm glad you ask. That is none other than the male. If you look and study the structure of your homes carefully over the last few years, you will see that there is an assault on the male Earth Dweller to either weaken him or remove him from the household entirely. Ultimately, he must be the one that has knowledge of my Commander and His words, and he must distribute it to all those within his home. But many men have failed this responsibility or have abdicated it altogether in search of other things. Both male and female are equally powerful, with equally different but vital responsibilities.

Ebenezer: Your adversary did not mention this when I questioned him.

MICHAEL: Indeed, he did not. Why would he? If he did, he would be unveiling one of his greatest strategies. One of, until now, his best-kept secrets.

Ebenezer: Certainly, this sheds light as to just how important this is to one's effectiveness. A very strategic move on his part. Mr. Prince, what do you say of this?

(Silence)

PRINCE: I choose to exercise my right and will remain silent on such a purposeless, frivolous question.

Ebenezer: Very well. Your silence on this matter speaks volumes. Michael, please continue. These "other things" you mention that have distracted many men. What type of distractions do you most commonly see?

MICHAEL: Ah, there are three distractions that I most commonly see that seek to influence and take control of all men. If one is able to avoid them, it is likely he has placed himself on good footing to fulfill his responsibility to not only himself but to his family and his generation as well. These three distractions my Commander most frequently refers to as "avidities." There is the ***avidity of the flesh***, the ***avidity of the eyes***, and the ***avidity of pride***. Are you familiar with these avidities?

Ebenezer: As you have described them, no, but perhaps I am just not understanding what exactly an "avidity" is, to begin with.

MICHAEL: An avidity, as I have described it, is simply hunger, eagerness, desire, or enthusiasm to an extreme. A person who is said to have an avidity for life is said to have within him an extreme hunger, desire, and enthusiasm for living. A man who possesses this within himself will do everything within his power to see to it that his life does, in fact, reflect that burning desire.

Ebenezer: So, a man with an avidity for the flesh does everything within his power to satisfy his body?

MICHAEL: Correct. A person with such a nature will stop at nothing to fulfill his sensual urges, even if it means breaking my Commander's first principles. This is a man who places pleasure over principle, a man who abuses the things that fulfill his sensual desires. These feelings and this pursuit become such a stronghold that he puts off all other responsibilities just to get it. He is willing to go to any length to quench the burning desires of his flesh. ***This is a man that will find himself, for lack of a better phrase, continuously compromising "so much" for "so little." A man who will continuously give away his power for "crumbs," even though he has been destined and created to have the "cake."***

Ebenezer: I understand. So, the man with an avidity for the flesh becomes so distracted that he puts off all effort to uplift and build up his family in a way that allows for his children to grow up in an environment conducive to giving their ultimate allegiance to your Commander. Noted. What is the second avidity, the avidity of the eyes, as you have stated? Please describe that as well in detail and provide an example.

MICHAEL: Yes, the second avidity is the ***avidity of the eyes***. In other words, a man develops an extreme desire to acquire the things he sees around him. It could be anything: a house, a car, a mate, or even smaller things, like collectibles such as trading cards, or coins, or stamps. Possessions are good; however, this individual has disordered his desire for them, placing them above everything else within his life, and just like the man who has an avidity for the flesh, this desire begins to dominate his thoughts and influence his actions. A man with an avidity for money will do everything and anything he can to acquire it, even oppressing the less fortunate and poor to attain it. He will live out this disordered priority by doing such things as working long hours at his job, or putting off family relationships and friendships, or spreading false information about a company through various mediums in order to influence the direction of a company's stock to his advantage.

Ebenezer: That last example is very specific, I might say. Very, very specific.

MICHAEL: Yes! This seems like a very common practice by you Earthlings as of late! It is rooted in an avidity for possessions and things. And remember, it is this extreme desire that takes a man out of position to be effective in dealing with the affairs of his home.

Ebenezer: Your adversary mentioned the banking system as a system with a deep desire to gain and acquire riches. Do you see this as the avidity of the eyes at work?

MICHAEL: My adversary here was making a diagnosis based on his assessment of the overall system as he sees it. Within that system, it is likely that there are men who have developed an insatiable desire to acquire possessions, including money, and that has influenced their decisions.

Ebenezer: And has then had an impact on his responsibility to his family. To keep it in line and on track to building a solid foundation for the children within the home to develop an allegiance from a young age to your Commander.

MICHAEL: That is very much the case. Can you think of other scenarios where a man might be influenced by such an avidity?

Ebenezer: Well, I know of not a few men who view members of the opposite sex as mere possessions. Within my daily circle, I know of such men, and in this age I live in, I believe it'd be hard to find a man that ***hasn't*** struggled at one time with this avidity or has thoroughly contemplated acting out its urges. Therefore, I can say with confidence based on your definition that quite a few have developed an avidity of the eyes as it relates to gaining the love of women so that they might become their possessions.

MICHAEL: That is a perfect example. Some of you earth-dwelling men have acquired some three, four, or five different women and treat them no better than the car you park in your driveway. When people are treated as mere possessions and things, this is a sure sign of this avidity.

Ebenezer: Ouch. I suppose, at times, one may forget that your Commander sees and hears all that is done on our Earth…

MICHAEL: Oh, yes. There is nothing that's hidden. You earth-dwelling men, always compromising so much for so little, settling for crumbs when you were destined to have the cake. What else?

Ebenezer: Uhhh…

MICHAEL: I am a bit concerned if you can only mention two…

Ebenezer: Why would this give you concern? It is not an easy thing for a man to be put on the spot like this. Pressure can make a fool of us all.

MICHAEL: Because if you understand the tactics of my adversary fully, you will understand that he uses and reuses these strategies each and every day to sway men like you off course. ***Remember, the reality you see hinges on moral principles; the reality you see has spiritual control.*** It is top priority that you see his tactics as they happen and be on your guard at all times, deflecting what he attempts to feed you with my Commander's first laws. But you are not wrong in that assessment…

Ebenezer: Which assessment?

MICHAEL: That pressure makes fools of many of you Earth Dwellers!

Ebenezer: Well, I'm glad I am correct about something! To test my luck, I will take a stab at the last avidity you have mentioned: the ***avidity of pride***. I would assume this simply deals with a man's desire to feel special and important and to be recognized by his peers for his work.

MICHAEL: I can simplify that just a bit to anything that causes a man to boast in himself. That is the extreme desire of the avidity of pride. This is a tricky one because as an Earth Dweller created in the image of my Commander, excellence is a part of his nature, and it is also a part of his nature to recognize the work he has created as being good. However, without proper deflection of that praise away from himself, he is at risk of developing a sense of pride that it was his own strength and his own power and might that brought about that excellence.

Ebenezer: Michael, what you have just stated has got my mind spinning once again in many different directions. There are many men who lift themselves up and boast in their own ability to achieve great things. What percentage of us earth-dwelling men do you see as struggling with this avidity?

MICHAEL: Many.

Ebenezer: How many?

MICHAEL: Billions.

Ebenezer: How many billions?

MICHAEL: Essentially, every man at one point or another has struggled with this avidity, most of them unknowingly. Just because one cannot see the struggle does not mean that it isn't there. It is the man's job to constantly analyze and reflect on his internal world and desires to keep in check this avidity to boast in himself.

Ebenezer: Is there any specific group of Earth Dwellers that you would say struggle with this the most?

MICHAEL: All those who carry an audience struggle to a great extent with this avidity, and it usually destroys them. For the sake of specifics, however, I would point to the entertainment system and the glory that other Earthlings bestow on the individual who excels and succeeds in effectively operating in his gifts within those realms. It is difficult for a man to avoid the avidity of pride when hundreds of thousands, sometimes millions of people, are screaming his name, regardless of whether he or she pledges his allegiance to my Commander.

Ebenezer: I find it interesting that you mentioned that your adversary was after this same type of praise but never received it. He wanted such glory to go to him as opposed to your Commander, and that was why he was removed from his position. Is that correct?

MICHAEL: That is right. The same type of glory that men must caution themselves and guard themselves against is the same glory that my adversary sought that did not and does not belong to him…

Ebenezer: I see. So this, too, is one of your tricks, Mr. Prince.

PRINCE: "Trick" is such a strong word. I call this true freedom. When a man is truly free, he is free to receive any type of praise that he desires, and he can either take the praise for himself or give it to someone else if he so chooses. What can be so wrong with that?

Ebenezer: According to your Adversary, everything. Nevertheless, to summarize Michael, a man must be on guard at all times for these avidities you have mentioned. In doing so, he positions himself in such a way that he can remain undistracted by the avidities of the world designed to take him out of alignment with his true responsibility with and for his family? To lead them in a way that places your Commander's principles as the guiding light for their lives?

MICHAEL: Your summary is accurate; however, remember that the man may, at times, fail to do this effectively, and as a matter of fact, in the current state of your Earth as I know it, it is a difficult thing to do, which is why constant self-analysis is critical for effective living.

Ebenezer: I must confess; I've been guilty at times of doing such, of "***compromising so much for so little, and settling for the mere crumbs of life when I was destined to have the cake,***" as you say. At times, it has been hard. But I strive each day to be better... (Pause) Anyway... I have heard much about the Earth in which I live from both you and your adversary. All this talk concerning it has created within me a desire to learn more about the country in which you're from, where your Commander resides. What is life like in that country?

MICHAEL: The celestial?

Ebenezer: The *celestial*?

MICHAEL: Yes, the celestial. That is another name for the Heavenlies, the country where my Commander resides.

Ebenezer: Ah, I see. So, I am correct in my reference to it as a country?

MICHAEL: Absolutely. As a matter of fact, I am quite taken back that you did. Most Earth Dwellers see it as some esoteric, mystical place when in reality, it's as real as the Earth where they live.

Ebenezer: I can't say that I've never fallen prey to such thoughts. But now is as good a time as ever to talk about it then, so I can relay to other yearning men the absolute truth. So, what is day-to-day life like up there?

MICHAEL: Everything in the Heavenlies reflects the Commander's nature. In other words, His lifestyle completely engulfs our lifestyle. First and foremost, when you enter into the Heavenlies through the gaining of citizenship, my Commander immediately takes away whatever history you had before and gives you a new one. That means that every man's sin, his degradation and abuse, his depression, sickness, and anxiety, is stripped and ripped away, and it is replaced with a new history reflecting his country—one of salvation, and peace, and joy, and love, and longsuffering, and goodness, and kindness—and He completely adopts you as one of His sons or daughters.

Ebenezer: Anxiety for peace? That sounds like a good deal to me! How does one gain membership, then, into the Heavenlies?

MICHAEL: Membership isn't given in order for one to enter the Heavenlies. The Heavenlies operates under a process of citizenship, as I stated… the same way your earthly country operates off of citizenship.

Ebenezer: Interesting. So, anyone can become a citizen of the Heavenlies as long as they qualify?

MICHAEL: That is correct. There is no exclusivity.

Ebenezer: That is much different than our earthly systems, where every man or woman can become a member in certain groups of his or her choosing.

MICHAEL: Much different. A broken system, in my opinion. How many different groups do you currently have, all claiming to carry the truth? And you should know, by the way, if you haven't already read between the lines, that ***it is*** possible to gain citizenship in the Heavenlies, even while you are still on Earth.

Ebenezer: And therefore, I can receive the benefits you mentioned?

MICHAEL: Correct. A completely new history.

Ebenezer: I am enjoying the sound of this more and more. What else can I know, or should I know, about the Heavenlies? What are the houses and streets like up there?

MICHAEL: If you want to better understand what the Heavenlies looks like, take a look around at the basic structure of your community and your world. What types of things do you see in your own city? Every city has land, language, laws, symbols, a constitution, a moral code, shared values, customs, social norms, and culture.

Ebenezer: I see. Then I would very much like to go there one day.

MICHAEL: Why?

Ebenezer: Why not?

MICHAEL: The Heavenlies is dangerous.

Ebenezer: What?

MICHAEL: I said ***the Heavenlies is dangerous***. It seems to be causing many of the problems for you Earth Dwellers here on Earth. The majority of the petitions we receive involve, in one way or another, the Heavenlies.

Ebenezer: I don't understand. You just stated that the Heavenlies is full of peace, and joy, and longsuffering, and love, and goodness, and kindness. How can that be bad?

MICHAEL: Because the Heavenlies promises you Earth Dwellers what you are inherently seeking.

Ebenezer: And what is that?

MICHAEL: Power and control over your environment. That is every Earth Dweller's search. But it's not without warrant. Most Earth

Dwellers, as we have discussed, are not living out their purpose, and they find themselves in a miserable existence under the control of many forces. They own nothing, including their time, their talent, nor their treasure. They live in constant fear and anxiety, unsure of what tomorrow will bring. Therefore, the idea of a place free from all of that stuff becomes their driving motive. Do you recall what we discussed concerning the relationship between the Heavenlies and you Earth Dwellers?

Ebenezer: Yes. Whatever us Earth Dwellers allow, the Heavenlies would allow. And whatever us Earth Dwellers do not allow, the Heavenlies would not allow.

MICHAEL: Correct. This is very important. Notice that those on Earth have full control over what transpires on Earth. Remember, you are a free-willed thinking agent, and the completion of your destiny, in all reality, has been placed in your own hands.

Ebenezer: As I think about it, most of my friends and relatives find themselves stressed out and fearful over the things they cannot control. Indeed, I can see how there is much validity in what you are saying.

MICHAEL: It is only the truth! If only a few men would take the truth and believe it and apply it, it would make my job much easier. And more fun, too. We would be opening up and unlocking many of the beautiful things stored up in the Heavenlies for you Earth Dwellers to access and enjoy on your Earth.

Ebenezer: If only a few men?

MICHAEL: Yes! It would transform your world overnight. I guarantee it. A few good leaders could go a long way in shaping your world. I'll give an example. In your car, there are thousands upon thousands of components. The ignition, the battery, the generator, the terminal wire, and the steering wheel are different, are they not? The same goes for all parts of the vehicle. Each part has a specific job as well. But they all have ***specific*** functions. But the key lies in the Earth Dweller knowing that function, knowing who he is, what part of the car he is. Remember, ***purity, power, persistence, petition, purpose, and potential.*** Purpose and potential are directly related to who you are as an individual—or which part of the car you are. When an Earth Dweller does not know his purpose or potential, his leadership is inauthentic, and he must continue to perform rather than truly live. Many Earth Dwellers are basing their entire lives on other people's opinions. If you think hard, I am sure you will be able to think of quite a few who live in such a way.

Ebenezer: Trust me, Michael, I don't need to think too hard. Several come to mind straight away. Mr. Prince, I have heard about the Heavenlies, and now I would like to know where you reside. What is the place like where you make your home? Describe it for me.

PRINCE: Of course. I will tell you exactly where and what it is like…

What has no touch yet always causes quiver?
What makes his home in the warmest place so as to never cause a shiver?
What lacks aroma and yet can smell itself and all around it?
What comes and goes but never departs, remaining with those that found it?
What lies with most yet fails to get its rest?
What can limit contribution, even warring 'gainst the best?

What keeps two binded yet holds no rope to bound?
What finds itself pervasive, where the storage of money and wealth can all be found?
What makes one roar with laughter and at the same time want to weep?
What keeps a thing at shore though it dreams of casting deep?

What waits at every corner yet cannot be seen or heard?
What remains in one position but yet soars just like a bird?
What screams in time of war but yet fails to make a sound?
What rises to different levels but yet remains fixed upon the ground?

What robs of precious time but yet always gives it back?
What shuns discrimination, no matter white or black?

Ebenezer: I have not the slightest clue as to how to even begin to solve this. Perhaps you can provide a hint, or better yet, another riddle?

PRINCE: That is the only riddle I will be giving. Thank you.

Ebenezer: Michael, do you know?

MICHAEL: Yes, I believe I know the answer; however, it would benefit you greatly to crack the code for this yourself. The truth, once you find it, will always be yours, and no Earth Dweller will be able to take it away from you.

Chapter 11

Earth

—

December 31, 2019

Ebenezer: (Sighs) Why must this be so difficult? Let me move away from the poet and back to you, Michael. I have another question that I would like to inquire of you.

MICHAEL: Ask away.

Ebenezer: If your Commander is omniscient, or all-knowing as some would call it, it means He is aware of what will happen in both the near-and-long-term future. Correct?

MICHAEL: That is correct.

Ebenezer: Okay, so if He has that ability, then every moment of every day is simply a replay of the past-present that your Commander had already orchestrated. Is that not a fact?

MICHAEL: That is a fact, but remember that although my Leader's purposes never change, the plant to bring about that purpose may. My Commander, He sees the end from the beginning. And then He presses "play" on life, in a sense, to bring about the end He desires.

Ebenezer: And yet we Earth Dwellers still have and maintain the ability to decide.

MICHAEL: Of course! As I have stated, plans may change, but purpose never changes. An incredible gift from my Commander to you Earth Dwellers, the ability to will freely, I'd say.

Ebenezer: Explain to me this, then. We Earth Dwellers, as you call us, most of the ones I know, are constantly obsessed about the future—about life 10, 15, or 20 years from now, and what our lives will reflect when the present passes and those days come about. I, too, have found myself wrestling with this idea. So, I bid the two of you this question: Which is more important, the past, the present, or the future?

PRINCE: ***I will give you the truth as I see it. Anything less is a threat to your freedom.*** Without a doubt, the past and the future are equally as important for the Earth Dweller to focus all of his mental faculties on.

Ebenezer: And you, Michael, what would you say?

MICHAEL: The present is really the thing that matters most. And I find that too many of you Earth Dwellers align yourselves with the thinking of my adversary, I might add.

Ebenezer: Mr. Prince, you say the past and the future, but Michael says the present. At once, the two of you must defend your differing positions.

PRINCE: The Earth Dweller's glory depends upon his total body of work and the things he accumulates while living on this Earth. If he finds himself concerned only about the present, then what ability does he possess to plan and map out his future and his destiny? And if he finds himself only occupied with the here and now, then how is he able to make up for the mistakes of his past? If he isn't even aware of them? Both the past and the future are of equal importance. An Earth Dweller who is not concerned with either will face difficulty and troubles that will leave him unfulfilled in his endeavors.

MICHAEL: I would be careful with this little devil. Remember, he is a crafty little thing, indeed. If a man is concerned about his past, it is because he is operating out of his own strength—he must remember it for fear of repeating it again. If an Earth Dweller is concerned about his future, it is because he is operating out of his own strength as well, for he must establish every little detail to bring about the desired end. Both are equally dangerous. But if a man is focused on the present, it means that the stress of his future and the weight of his past are not up to him, but up to something or Someone greater that can lead him to where he should be.

Ebenezer: I assume that something or Someone happens to be your Commander?

MICHAEL: The way He has designed it, an Earth Dweller cannot live fully at all if he finds himself unable to live fully now.

Ebenezer: This seems like a trap of sorts to me, if I may be honest. We have been given free will and have been blessed with the ability to think rationally, and yet it is to our detriment to think in terms of either the future or the past?

MICHAEL: The *extremes* of the future or the past. There is nothing wrong with planning for your future or remembering old times with friends and loved ones, but to have those rob you of the gift of the present is a grave mistake.

Ebenezer: What should the present look like, then? What type of mentality should an Earth Dweller carry who is correctly in line with his priorities, as you state them?

MICHAEL: An Earth Dweller who finds himself fully perfected in abiding in the present has completely mastered the two principles of ***petition*** and ***power***. In everything he does, at every moment of every day, he is in constant communication with the Head Office. Everything he does is with this relationship in mind.

Ebenezer: I recall you stated earlier that the power within is a wonderful communicator and will act as the navigational system of our lives, alerting us as to when we are off or on course in terms of the direction we are heading.

MICHAEL: Precisely. Power appropriated by my Commander. And what about that petition?

Ebenezer: Petitioning, as you stated, is a human representing your Commander's rights on Earth. You stated that petition is necessary because your Commander's influence cannot come to Earth without it.

MICHAEL: Do you see how both of those have the potential to be continuously active states? Do you see how both require one to be fully present to what he is facing at the moment and not many years in the past or in the future? And do you see how it requires one to be fully aware of the here and now? This is the key. It is of tremendous use for you to look ahead or behind in this way, but you will fail to develop the deeper communion that my Commander wants to have with you today, here and now.

Ebenezer: I see. Why must the world put so much pressure, then, on us Earth Dwellers, or humans, to succeed? To arrive at a certain destination?

PRINCE: Allow me to interject so as to add some balance to this conversation. It is because it is absolutely necessary in order for each Earth Dweller to ensure he attains the glory and praise that he rightfully deserves. How can one strive to attain if he has not the destination of his life already fixed within his mind? How can one strive to overcome his past if he is not fully and completely aware of it at all times? How can one choose to make better choices if he is not constantly analyzing and contemplating his decisions in terms of either the past or the future? How can one know what money and material things will satisfy his soul if he does not look into the future fully and completely and plan for it?

Ebenezer: It does feel good to be recognized for my work. I certainly don't feel life has given me the praise and the good job that I've wanted for all of the work that I've done thus far. Michael, what do you say to this?

MICHAEL: Perhaps I should take you outside once again. Come with me.

Ebenezer: To where?

MICHAEL: Come with me. Take the recorder as well, please.

Ebenezer: Okay, is he coming? Mr. Prince.

PRINCE: Oh yes, I'm coming. I know exactly where we're going.

...

(Shuffling)

...

(Door Opens)

...

(Door Closes)

Ebenezer: I see my angels are still enjoying themselves under this early morning sky.

MICHAEL: Yes, hopefully, my men will be given something to do soon. Of that I am confident based on the knowledge you have now attained! See, you'll notice they will attend to you as you move. Give it a try using the principle of petition.

Ebenezer: Uh, okay. What should I say?

MICHAEL: Just ask my Commander to protect you on this short journey. Tell Him that He said He would give His angels complete charge over you to keep you in all your ways.

Ebenezer: Commander, please protect me on this trip. You said You would give Your angels charge over me to keep me in everything I do.

MICHAEL: There you go. How are you doing, my friends?

Ebenezer: Wow! That really worked. My bodyguards.

MICHAEL: Of course it worked.

Ebenezer: Amazing. How far down are we heading? We are getting closer and closer to the gated area and out of my neighborhood. It's just a few blocks down.

MICHAEL: I know. That's precisely where we are heading! There is one property, in particular, I want you to see.

PRINCE: Hee-hee.

Ebenezer: I hope to one day move to these parts.

MICHAEL: This, I know as well. We receive your petition every week up in the head office.

Ebenezer: You have? Then why haven't you answered yet?

MICHAEL: My friend, have you already forgotten the principle of purpose and petition that we discussed?

Ebenezer: That's right. Yes, I remember. My petition must align with your Commander's law and His principles that He intended to govern the Earth. If they align with those of your adversary's, then my law is out of harmony with your Commander's law, and my petition will not be answered.

MICHAEL: Does your request sound familiar?

Ebenezer: Familiar to...

MICHAEL: The avidities we discussed earlier.

Ebenezer: Hmm, I never thought about it in that way...

MICHAEL: Perhaps it may be time to think a bit differently.

...

(Footsteps)

...

MICHAEL: Here we are.

Ebenezer: An unfinished house…

MICHAEL: Correct. An ***unfinished*** house. But not just any unfinished house.

Ebenezer: What other types of unfinished houses are out there? I assume there is a lesson to be learned here as well.

MICHAEL: There are quite a few, and yes, this here is a ***tragically*** unfinished house. One replete with illusion and confusion.

PRINCE: Allow me to do the honors by telling it, for it is a fantastic story. You see, through many of my wonderful principles, I was able to convince this man that all of my dreams were his dreams. From the time he was in grade school, I began to push him and overwhelm him with the belief that he must begin at once in climbing the ladder of life—the ladder of success and accomplishment that would set him on a path toward gaining the greater things in this life, the external things that so awesomely define my kingdom. From first grade to the second, I weathered him with my ideals, beating him down day by day through my many mediums the idea of one day "arriving" at a life destination. On from the second grade this young man went, on to middle school and then to high school. He took the accelerated courses, graduating with a perfect average and earning the title of valedictorian of his class. An eloquent graduation speech he gave. He did this all with the hope of one day ***arriving***. So, the story continues, the young man was good enough to get into a top-five college, where he was a double major, excelling in both the classroom and intramural sports. Instead of graduating in four, he did it in three, all the while avoiding one of my master's subtle pitfalls that capture many of you Earth Dwellers, debt. Commendable. However, my master and I were completely at ease with this because I knew I already had him. He was far along already on my wonderful path of regret. So, after graduating at a very young age, he took another step on the ladder before him, and he continued his climb into the real world, going into business for himself, breaking the six-figure mark in net revenue only three years after graduation. A phenomenal feat. It was then I began to hand him the other wonderful riches his hands had earned; he had the cars, the vacations, and the relational command that would be the envy of even the great emperors of old. But it was not enough; it couldn't be enough. He still had much more of the gamut to climb. So onward he went, climbing life's skyscraping ladder, reaching higher and higher for the wonderful stars. More money, a bigger house, more power…

MICHAEL: The avidities of life…

PRINCE: Something of that nature! Onward and onward he went, grasping and reaching, trying to outdo his peers and his friends, all the while putting aside his family.

(Silence)

Ebenezer: And then what happened?

MICHAEL: A familiar pattern. He simply got tired of reaching. Or rather, he ***realized*** he shouldn't be reaching. So, he made the decision to slow down, sell his business, and begin several philanthropic causes to give back to his community.

PRINCE: All great things, I suppose, in the eyes of my Adversary. But it was all too late, for he found himself riddled with infirmities and sickness—so much so that he no longer had the strength to give even half of himself to those causes. And all at the age of 55!

MICHAEL: Unfortunately, that is the truth. This man died, just last night, as a matter of fact, while still building this home. His "dream" home, the one that would lead him into the next phase of life—an existence of giving back and helping others. From kindergarten to first grade, second, third, and fourth. Then to high school and up the ladder to college and into the real world. He struggled long hours for "success" to climb the great and wonderful steps that my adversary strategically laid before him. He "arrived" at 45, but it was a foolish and tragic arrival. The man was always living for the future, to be somewhere he wasn't. The world called him a "visionary," but he was simply a man that had not learned how to take the time to enjoy his life. He planned for the future that he is no longer here to see.

Ebenezer: Just last night? You mentioned this man had a family? Surely, he was able to pass down some of his possessions to them.

MICHAEL: Yes, he had several children, and yes, he was able to pass along his wealth to them. But if that is a man's only definition of success, then he is tragically mistaken and is at risk of missing the full depth of his calling.

Ebenezer: Please, inform me!

MICHAEL: This man planned for a future that never arrived. He never enjoyed the fruits of all his labor. But even the fruit that he did bear was of little importance because he used it on himself. A man is not able to truly live unless he is able to live in the here and the now.

Ebenezer: Fifty-five. That is much too young. Did this man accomplish any of his purpose?

MICHAEL: That, in itself, is another tragedy. That man not only died prematurely, but because he believed my adversary's lies and fell victim to his distorted principles, his understanding of his true purpose became distorted as well. His true calling was not to simply accumulate many things or large piles of money; it was to begin doing what he had put off for more than 20 years.

Ebenezer: Is it possible for his children to complete that purpose for him? After all, they have now inherited and have his wealth in their possession.

MICHAEL: That is a great possibility; they could continue the work he was doing and bring about the end that was actually designed for their father. However, they, too, have their own responsibilities to fulfill their own purposes during their lifetimes. Another lesson to be learned is that my Commander gives purpose across generations, meaning that each generation is a continuation of the last, in a sense. Remember, plans may change, but purpose remains constant. But the man who never finished this house was never able to feel the satisfaction that the completion of his purpose could only bring him! Even if his children complete it for him, they are not him, and therefore, they will not gain that same level of satisfaction. This is a tragedy. A tragedy indeed.

Ebenezer: Mr. Prince, why would you seek to dupe a man in this way? Why would you trick him into thinking anything other than his purpose will satisfy him?

PRINCE: I have done no such thing. No such thing at all. Remember, I only offer the truth, the real truth, and anything else other than this truth is a threat to your freedom. Freedom that my Adversary seeks to take away.

Ebenezer: So, you didn't force this man to obey your principles?

PRINCE: Force? You should know by now that I can do no such thing to even the weakest of men. Every man possesses within him the power of choice and free will. Each man has the ability to decide which principles he will live by. If my Adversary is upset about only a small few obeying or adhering to His principles, then perhaps He should make the rewards of following them a bit more appealing! Wouldn't you say? Not a few men enjoy climbing my ladder in hopes of gaining the true riches of this world. Of obeying my principles wholeheartedly and steadfastly.

MICHAEL: He is correct; neither he nor my Commander can force any Earth Dweller to do as he says. It is up to the Earthling to decide which way his life should go. Remember this: many Earth Dwellers approve of the better things of life, but it is the evil things they still find themselves doing. Don't be discouraged if you relay this message to the world and it seems to fall on deaf ears. For they have rejected my Commander Himself, so they may also reject you.

Ebenezer: I will keep that in mind. As I look over everything that has been said here, I believe I have about as much information as I can handle at the moment, as all of my questions have been addressed, and then some. I am very satisfied, as no attempts were made by either you, Michael, or your adversary to avoid this interview in even the slightest sense. However, though it has been stated that something drastic is going to occur in the coming decade, and although I have the benefit of being able to look back at history, I still do not have the slightest clue as to what exactly will transpire that will prime individuals for the work that your adversary will do. Mr. Prince, do you have any final words on this?

PRINCE: First, I must confess that listening to this ogre has made me a bit agitated. And as I have said several times this evening, I have no responsibility to respond to any of the accusations that have been presented here today and to any questioning that goes beyond the scope of that written by my Adversary. Therefore, I will remain silent. But before I do, however, let me remind you that I am still, and will always be, the greatest caretaker of your freedom, and I have helped to give many millions of people the things that satisfy their sensual natures, allowing them to fully enjoy and revel in the labor they have put forth under the sun. Can there be anything better than true freedom?

Ebenezer: True freedom, I suppose, is a good thing.

PRINCE: Yes! Indeed, it is. Obeying my principles, remember, will be your key to true freedom.

Ebenezer: I will keep this in mind. You, too, Mr. Prince, like Michael here, seem to have taken on human form. You seem to be just a regular earthly being. From our conversation today, I understand now that it is likely that you have, in fact, taken possession of a human body. I will ask you again; please confirm where it is that you live and breathe and make your life in this form.

PRINCE: That, as I have said, shall remain anonymous! I have already provided you the clue that will tell you the very form of my nature and the description of the place where I reside. Do with the riddle as you wish.

Ebenezer: You are a stubborn one. Michael, is there anything you would like to add before I end this recording?

MICHAEL: Principles, Ebenezer. Principles. Principles. Principles. First laws. ***Remember, the reality you see hinges on moral principles, and the reality you see has spiritual control.*** This is a direct word from my Commander at the Head Office. Communicate this experience and warn all those of what is coming in the next decade. If you follow the principles I have shared with you, the world and humankind will be just fine. That being said, related to the world and humankind, I must add, there is one last principle that I have not yet shared. It is the ***principle of people***. It is impossible to win the war against my adversary without all of the potential of each and every individual walking the face of the Earth. Each person has a wealth of capability to complete his purpose, that if manifested, would rip control of the systems of the Earth from the clutches of my adversary and into the hands of the kingdom of light. So, people, Ebenezer, don't forget the people. Tell all who will hear of what is coming by my adversary and be on guard at all times of his wily tricks, for he is out to deceive at all times.

Ebenezer: I don't think one can have such an experience as this and not tell others about what has been seen or heard! But will the people listen? According to you, they may not.

PRINCE: The answer to that would be a resounding no! In fact, the reason I feel so comfortable divulging so much as I sit across from you today is that I know that the minute you tell your fellow Earthlings about this conversation, they will soon write you off as crazy and a man of unsound mind. For most of the men you know of are already under my influence! So, go ahead. Print and distribute it as you wish throughout the entire world. Then watch your reputation go down to the lowest depths of the grave, never to rise again. Watch what will be disseminated about you in all of the mediums that I control.

Ebenezer: Your true colors have now risen to the surface, Mr. Prince.

MICHAEL: Ebenezer, don't be intimidated by this little devil. Remember, you have at your disposal a set of protectors serving a government ready to back you up at all costs. You can call on them at any time to protect you, as long as you voice the Commander's word. Be aware of his principles and don't succumb to them. ***Guard your mind at all costs.***

Ebenezer: Thank you, Michael. How do you suggest I get this word to the masses?

MICHAEL: That is up to you; however, I would suggest you make it unconventional, whatever route that may be. It is better to have one or two on fire and with passion for releasing this message than a million people lukewarm. But it was your request that brought us here this evening and into this late hour. Whatever you decide, remember, the Head Office will allow, and whatever you do not decide, the Head Office will deny. Remember, the kingdom of darkness is to destroy you. The kingdom of light is to give you life. Walk in the light. Light is knowledge. The kingdom of darkness gets its power from what you don't know. Keep reading, keep studying, keep gaining knowledge of the truth, and that will set you free from the forces of darkness. But also remember, no matter what you learn, if it isn't the word from my Commander, it will not destroy darkness. Now, I compel you, the power is in your hands as to how to communicate this information to your Earth to allow for its greatest impact. Choose wisely! Much is on the line!

Ebenezer: Very well. I will communicate it to the best of my ability. So, the principles we have discussed today include purity, power, persistence, petition, purpose, potential, and people. We have also discussed the avidities, as you have coined them. I will keep these close to my chest. Gentlemen, ***thank you.***

(Recording Ends)

This concluded my meeting with Asbeel, "Prince of Air," and Michael, "Chief Archangel of the Heavenlies," on December 31, 2019.

Chapter 12

—

And so went my interview with these two very interesting gentlemen. I escorted them to the vehicle that I assumed belonged to the little round fellow, the van with the inscription "Prince of Air" plastered on the side. The three of us walked gingerly toward it in the cold morning night, Michael commenting on the orderliness of the neighborhood right before parting ways with his men who had been waiting in the streets as my guardian angels. Asbeel said no words, appearing to be somewhat distraught, and simply hopped into the driver's seat as Michael got in as the passenger, buckled himself in, and sped off into the night. I was left standing there by myself, for as I turned, even my guardians that I had once seen were now gone. I was there all alone, standing in the middle of the street, halfway under a street floodlight. Realizing how ridiculous it may have looked to others to be by myself, still in my pajamas at such an early hour of the morning, I made my way back to my ajar door and shut it carefully behind me.

Upon entering my house, I first returned to the table where we had seated to ensure I still had the recording of our interview intact. The recorder was still there. Then, to ensure that the contents of the interview were still present, I pressed the play button, and the voices of both men again filled the four walls of my kitchen. Though still in a little disbelief, wondering if I was, in fact, dreaming, I carefully climbed the stairway to my home and reentered my bedroom, all the while peeping through my window a few more times to ensure there were no more "guardians" sitting in my driveway. All I could see was the neighborhood cat scurrying across my yard.

I removed my slippers and crawled back into bed, still clutching the recorder. I must admit that sleep, again, escaped me that early morning, as one would expect if he was to have had such an encounter. So really, I lay wide awake in the comfort of my bed until sometime later when I began to see the slightest ray of early morning sun shining through my bedroom window.

At once, I began the process of transferring and transcribing the interview down to paper. What you have just read was how I had typed it in its entirety. There were, of course, instances where the recorder did not pick up the highest sound quality, such as our time in the other neighborhood, so I have done my best to recall the conversation and dialogue in its completeness as well. Sadly, and all the more adding to the oddness of the situation, upon the transfer of the dialogue the next day, I could no longer rewind and replay the conversation. Once I had listened and transferred its contents over, the audio recording of it was gone. What remained was heavy static where the voices of the two men had, at one time, been heard.

Nonetheless, of course, as Michael had mentioned, the purpose for the interview was not merely for education, but for action; not for entertainment, but for information that could and would provide actionable and practical steps to assist human beings in the coming decade. And as he had stated, the interview was in response to my very own inquiry I had raised some weeks ago. I have read through the letter containing the questions again, and this is very much, despite a few departures, accurate. My only regret is that I did not have the presence of mind to ask each man more. Nevertheless, several key moments have stood out to me as I have since reflected on what both men stated. All of which can be encompassed under the giant and eclectic umbrella of ***war***. Yes, you read that correctly, ***war***. That is the only word I have come to conclude that is adequate to define it, and as each day passes, I perceive more and more the truths from both sides, and I am more and more aware of each man's intentions as they relate to us humans breaking ground into the new decade.

Before I dive into my assessment at a much deeper level at the end of this writing, I would like to first inform you of a brief experience that had come about only a few days following the interview. I was sitting at my office desk in my upstairs area when suddenly, the lights throughout all of the upstairs rooms went completely out. I did my best but had no luck in getting them up and working again, so I took my assignments downstairs into my den, where I placed my feet up on the coffee table as I worked through the coming week's workload.

Shortly after that, I received a phone call from a dear friend telling me to turn the television to the regional news, stating that there was a developing story of great national significance. The request seemed odd, especially coming from this particular friend, but I obeyed, flipping on the television and clicking through channels until I reached the evening regional news. It was nearing the end of the hour, and the reporter was now transitioning to sign off of the air. He was informing the public that Americans should begin "preparing for precautionary measures by city and local governments to halt the spread of an infectious agent that had been slowly spreading throughout the country," mirroring what had been occurring worldwide over the previous several weeks.

At first, I listened carefully as he continued; however, as the man went on, I slowly began to doze—my interest beginning to wane as he'd begun to talk in what seemed to be an endless amount of circles. Finally, the man reached the point where he was interrupted by the news team in the studio as they carefully interjected, alerting him of the need to finalize his story. But what he said in the ensuing moments shocked me, so much so that it sent a chilling spike down my spine. I believed I ceased breathing for something close to a minute. You see, the reporter had now split the screen simultaneously with the others in the studio, and the men at the desk began to banter with him regarding the detail of his closing statement, making a joke about the level of precision in which he had mirrored the leadership of the country. As they said their final goodbyes, the man at the desk calmly looked into the camera and tried to bring some seriousness back into the equation by saying reassuringly:

"In spite of all the banter here at Channel 9, we always strive to offer you the truth, the real truth—because we believe that anything else is simply a threat to your freedom."

My mouth just about dropped and hit the floor as I heard this, and so I immediately called my friend back and asked if he had heard the newscaster sign off of the air.

"Yeah, I heard it. What about it?" he replied.

"Did you hear the last part, about freedom?" I asked.

"Yes, I heard it—what's so special about that? That's what ***ALL*** the news channels say these days, in one way or another."

Up to that point, I hadn't told anyone of my encounter with the two gentlemen, as any reasonable person could understand why, so to him, the statement didn't make the least bit of sense. But to me, I immediately thought about the little round fellow and the goliath of a man sitting patiently at my table as I carefully peppered each with questions. I thought about the fact that this could be the beginning of what the little goblet called his "plans for the coming future." Perhaps his intentions for the world and for the coming decade were quietly unfolding now.

Chapter 13

The Heavenlies

—

"So, you see, Mr. Bigsby, the storehouses in the WOH building operate in a unique kind of way. They can only be opened and their contents disbursed when an Earth Dweller activates a principle set in motion by the Boss. Giving is that principle. When an Earth Dweller gives on Earth, it makes us angels pretty busy in that building. Many Earth Dwellers are shocked when they see the amount of stuff they could have appropriated on Earth, but because they never operated under that principle, they simply left it untapped.

"I see," Mr. Bigsby said, thinking about his own life he had just lived on Earth. Quite embarrassed and a little regretful, he quickly changed the subject. "So, where are we off to next?" he asked.

"Off to meet the Commander. He'd really like to see you. He wants to give you another chance," Netzach said.

Mr. Bigsby slowed his pace, and his mind began racing, not exactly sure what Netzach really meant. Before he could think on the matter much longer, however, he noticed an even larger group of seraphim exiting another building just across the streets of crystal-clear gold. Oddly enough, as the seraphim mingled amongst themselves just outside the building, a few of them pointed in Mr. Bigsby's direction and appeared to be talking amongst themselves. Mr. Bigsby was confused.

"Netzach, sorry for all the questions, but what are all of those seraphim doing over there on the other side? The ones standing outside of that building?" he asked.

"The one over there? Oh, that's another popular building here known as the 'Spectacle Theatre.' Inside, we angels can get a direct, front-row view of what's happening on Earth at any particular moment in time. Usually, an angel can choose to watch some of the most important events taking place at the time. Essentially, you Earth Dwellers are center stage, and the seraphim are the audience sitting in the stands. We can observe all activities, we can hear conversations, and we can gain wisdom by watching the events play out. The Theatre is one of my favorite places to be, I might add, for it allows me to see many of the awesome things that tend to happen on Earth.

"I see. Any idea what they just finished playing?" Mr. Bigsby asked. "Looks like it got a pretty big crowd."

"A huge crowd--I've never seen anything like it. But I'm not surprised. Today was an interesting day on Earth. One of our most powerful angels has been down there escorting one of the adversary's minions at the request of the Boss. Usually, those types of scenarios only last a few minutes, but this one has gone on for hours. And I hear they even took a field trip or two outside into those streets. I think they went to look at some houses or something.

Mr. Bigsby's mind was now spinning. There was so much to the Heavenlies that it was hard to fathom. Nevertheless, he continued pacing Netzach, and the two made their way down the crystal-clear streets of gold next to the flowing river and in the direction of the bright, beaming light, which became brighter and brighter the closer the two got to it. After a few more strides, it was just a few paces away, and Netzach suddenly stopped. Mr. Bigsby could hear voices singing, growing to higher and higher octaves.

The closer the two got to the light, the more peace and love he felt within him. It was a calming feeling that was rushing over him that he never wanted to end. Even stranger, he became aware, was the fact that the more he went in the direction of the vibrancy, the clearer the strategies and ideas became in his mind for the things he could have done, and perhaps should have done, on Earth. A part of him, it seemed, even longed for the opportunity to fulfill them, and he hoped that his new home in the Heavenlies would afford him that possibility—to build what he should have built but never acted upon on Earth.

Oh well. Now I'm in the Heavenlies, he thought to himself as the two continued on their way directly into the light, off to meet the King.

***

Earth

I, Ebenezer, found myself again dozing off on my couch, a pool of drool streaming down my chin, the weariness of the last few days overtaking my physical body. I had solved the riddle, and I felt as prepared as I ever had for the events that were to come in the future. Though still a bit tired, there was a peace I now felt that hadn't been there for some time. A part of me wondered if there would ever be a place that would allow this feeling to remain in abundance forever, not just in passing. As I thought on these things, I again turned my attention toward my television, where a breaking story was just unfolding. I carefully sat up straight and inched forward on my couch, not believing in the slightest the amazing news I was hearing. I quickly turned the volume up on my television as the studio reporter began to speak.

"In recent news, a local man who was medically pronounced dead for more than 24 hours was brought back to life, and doctors are claiming it is nothing short of a medical miracle. The man, just 55 years old, showing no signs of the incurable sickness that had taken his life, has now embarked on a mission, he states, that will solely be focused on giving and impacting the world and the community around him. And now this "Miracle Man" seems to be putting his money where his mouth is, selling the dream home he claims he'd been building over the last several years in a beautiful, gated community and investing those proceeds into local for-profit businesses focused on eradicating the cities problems. A truly incredible story that we'll hear much more about after the break."

Epilogue

—

Now, before you close this book and begin to ponder its pages, I must move forward and discuss several of my takeaways—perhaps you may perceive them differently, which is very fine with me. I believe it is the intention of Michael's Commander that such be so in allowing the interview, for it was His hope that the message would be disseminated and shared with every single Earth Dweller who is living within the planet's systems.

War: An Interesting Umbrella

War, as I see it and will define it here, is the state of open and declared hostile armed conflict between states and nations. It is a period defined by armed discord and can also be expressed as a state of hostility, dissension, or antagonism that occurs between opposing forces for a particular end.

With this definition as my foundation, in my own opinion, two things regarding Michael and Asbeel have become increasingly clear: The two opposing sides are, first and foremost, in a bitter war with one another. Both men did not hide the fact that each side, Michael's Commander and Asbeel's master, were engaging in declared and open hostile conflict since the beginning of creation. And secondly, it is also abundantly clear that it had led to a state of hostility over one specific end—the ascent and supremacy of the principles by which each side governed. This is the umbrella through which all other things are filtered. Asbeel's master, as Michael mentioned, declared war on Michael's Commander when his quest for glory and power trumped his allegiance to his Adversary, and the ensuing rebellion established an opposing governmental entity—the kingdom of darkness. It wasn't long after that Asbeel and his master began to deploy a simple military strategy to overthrow their new enemy.

But what strategy?

Military strategy can be defined as the planning and conduct of campaigns, the movement and disposition of forces, and the aim to deceive the enemy. That is exactly what Asbeel and his master began to do as they deployed this strategy against the first man and woman in the garden. As Asbeel admitted, this strategy includes a weighted focus toward isolation and independence, both creating the fertile ground for such an insidious military campaign to gain legs and take root. As time has passed, that stratagem has evolved, and its roots have run deeper, to the point that, at an eye glance, it is nearly impossible to perceive its influence. However, as I have now seen, partly because my own eyes have been opened, his master has weaseled his arms around the most effective mediums to disseminate and transfer his ideals. That would explain the statement from my story on Channel 9. Admittedly, that tactical strategy, I have come to wholeheartedly believe, is where he spends the majority of his time.

In terms of other specific strategies, I have come to conclude from the round little fellow's responses that the breakdown of the family could be of much greater significance than each of us Earth Dwellers, at first glance, might actually think, and that this, too, is a strategic militaristic-like assault by the kingdom of darkness on the kingdom of light. So, what else has his master's government accomplished through such a strategy? Today, my research shows that not a small number of births occur to women who are single or living with a non-marital partner. Some even conclude that there is no longer one dominant family form in the United States. It was clear from the statements by Mr. Prince that one of his master's greatest war tactics involves gaining the influence of children from a very young age. One can imagine how alarmed I became upon hearing that not a few children younger than six had experienced a major change in their family or household structure, in the form of death, parental divorce, separation, marriage, or cohabitation. In other words, it would seem stability has taken its wings and flown off to a distant and far country, and inconsistency and chaos have perched and made their home in its place.

Fueling these statistics is the fact that Americans today are exiting marriages at higher rates than in the past. As Asbeel so bluntly put it: "Without 'healthy' family, as my Adversary sees it, there is no mission. And when there is no mission, there is no identity. And where there is no identity, a person becomes open to taking on the identity placed on him by other people, through various other mediums." Identity can be defined as the fact of being who or what a person or thing is. It is the characteristics determining who or what a person or thing is. It is derived from the Latin word ***idem***, which simply means "same."

It is here that we see just how toe-to-toe both sides have positioned themselves in this heated warfare. It is apparent to me that every assault by one side will be met by an equal attack by the other. For example, if Mr. Prince is sent to attack and tear apart the family structure, then Michael has been sent to protect it; if Mr. Prince has been sent to disperse his tricks and lies through various mediums, then Michael and his men seek and hope to disseminate the truth. If Mr. Prince's aim is to destroy purpose and destiny, then Michael and his Commander seek to preserve and protect it. Under those terms and through that lens, it may be that even a blind man can see just how bloody the warfare has become and can be, for at each and every waking hour of every day, there is somewhat of a constant jostling between the two for position within the systems of Planet Earth.

This brings me to another critical takeaway that can be classified under this umbrella I call war: The systems of Earth are the battlegrounds for all of this activity. How easily and unassumingly have

I gone about my day-to-day life paying no attention to each of these systems that both gentlemen discussed! I blindly turned my eyes to the level of warfare taking place within them. I have resolved since the interview to keep, at all times, the awareness that with every action, I am contributing to either government's campaign in its struggle for ultimate control. There is no neutrality in such, for even in silence, a sense of betrayal still remains, and even in one's non-allegiance, he is really expressing his allegiance based on the principles that are at play.

Thus, my final takeaway is in regard to these principles, or first laws, that both Mr. Prince and Michael mentioned. For adherence to first laws, I have concluded, as you may have as well, seems to be at the core of the constant struggle. The military might that can effectively use its strategy to establish first laws will ultimately wield full control over the other side's government. But surprisingly, as you may have read, neither government can completely and unrestrainedly force its will over humankind and the Earth in totality. The decision to allow for any government to wield its unrestricted control belongs in the hands of the Earth Dwellers, you and me. We decide which principles we follow and which ones we ultimately reject. We decide how strong or weak our families become by the principles we adhere to. We decide whether our children grow up in a place where they are nurtured and cared for based on the unique gifts and emotional involvement of each parent, or in isolated darkness, leading to confusion in their ultimate purpose and identity. We decide whether the focus of our lives will lead us down the long and dark corridor of the accumulation of things for only our personal enjoyment, rather than the accumulation of things so that we can, in turn, help our fellow man. We decide. And that in itself is the greatest challenge but also the greatest opportunity. Both you and I know which course we are on. Our destiny, which was established before the beginning of time, is uniquely in our hands.

As the days have passed, I have been ruminating on this idea that each and every day, a battle is being fought between two opposing forces, two opposing governments, and that each is on a relentless quest to establish its laws within the systems of the Earth. Specifically, the following contrasting statements from my interview stand out to me as carrying great weight for this discussion:

MICHAEL: Freedom means one seeks to control his own behavior, without the coercion of external forces such as government.

PRINCE: In true freedom, external coercion and control are necessary to maintain a functioning society!

How profound are these statements! At first glance, these contrasting ideas may not seem as much, but both carry dynamic meanings. I mentioned earlier that we alone decide which principles or laws we follow, which is very much true in the physical world but even more true in the invisible world. It is just as true in the natural as in the supernatural. It is just as relevant in the world that we cannot see as it is in the world that we can. For example, think back to the principle of protection that Michael stated was available to each man, but very few men used—protection through His protective agents. When we call on them and order them on guard to protect us, they must adhere to our word if we are under proper authority with the heavenly government. This *is* the supernatural. In the natural sense, if we as Earth Dwellers are facing issues and we pick up the phone to dial the local authorities, just as I first intended to do upon the initial arrival of the two complete strangers at my door, the police must act on the citizens' behalf to protect them. Therefore, in this case, the natural very much is comparable to the supernatural.

Now with that said, the prolific thinker Henry David Thoreau once stated in his essay ***Civil Disobedience***, "Government is best which governs least… Government is best which governs not at all; and that when men are prepared for it, that will be the kind of government which they will have."

In my honest and humble opinion, this statement alone provides the critical key to advancement in the new decade, the key to true purpose, and the key to living a fulfilling and abundant life. I believe it is the answer for which I was searching when I originally cried out and inquired about in my office those many evenings. It also has solidified to whom I shall pledge my own allegiance and whose principles I will strive to follow.

But why?

***

If government is best that governs least, it is because that external government is no longer needed to relegate a man or woman's behavior. In essence, the natural form of government that we have become accustomed to relying on minimizes, and the supernatural or spiritual form of government that too many of us have remained unfamiliar with maximizes. A man or woman polices himself and continues to monitor his own actions to the point that he does good simply because it is the right thing to do. He does right because it is right. He is honest in all of his dealings because it is right to be honest and just. Consequently, the government does not necessarily decide to govern least by decision; it simply is not needed to a greater extent because an internal law has become greater than the external law, and obedience to that internal law leads to the correct behavior externally. Men and women strive wholeheartedly to abide by an invisible law. They follow higher principles that go above and beyond external law, to the point where they adhere to principles that other men and women cannot see.

If government becomes an entity that continuously progresses to governing less, then eventually, as I have stated, that government may not need to govern at all. The key, however, is that this invisible law that man progressively adheres to is in alignment with the correct internal government—which is the battle that I have seen between Michael and Mr. Prince and that we have now discussed to a great extent. When an individual obeys the invisible laws of Mr. Prince and his master, it is my belief that external government must inevitably expand. When an individual obeys the invisible laws of Michael and his Commander, external government can be retracted. The will of man is responsible for what transpires in the external world, and the external world around us is simply an exact reflection of the internal world within us. We may find ourselves draped in wonderful, expensive attire, shoes immaculately polished, hair nicely done, but if the principles by which we live teeter on the side of Asbeel and his master, I have come to believe, then the external world in which we live will reflect that chaotic internal reality. As water reflects the face, so a man's life reflects his mind.

I must take this a step further, by referencing what Michael stated in very fine detail as it relates to the process of the acceptance of principles, which must be reiterated:

"Your mind receives information from your senses, and the information from your senses that goes into the mind is deposited into your soul. The soul is made up of your will and your emotions. Your soul then takes that information from your senses and deposits it into your spirit, which is the source of the power that I just discussed with you earlier. Your spirit, your body, and your soul are all interrelated. The soul receives from the spirit and discerns whether what it has received is right or not. This is where the power under which you find yourself influenced becomes of paramount importance. If what you are receiving from your senses is corrupt, meaning the principles are incorrect, then your soul will be damaged, and even if your spirit does not agree, it will be subject to your soul and the information that has been downloaded into it. So, the principle of purity is ensuring that what is received by the soul, body, and spirit are all aligned as one, integrated fully with the intentions of the one in whose allegiance you follow."

In other words, the spirit of the man may be in proper allegiance with Michael's Commander; however, if the principles he is exposed to and deposits into his soul are incorrect, then the man will still find himself living out of those corrupt principles. This, I have come to believe, is more fact than fiction. So, in all reality, the battle is one of principles—those principles seeking to influence the soul of the individual.

As I pondered the consequences of such, I came to believe that there is one thing I must do in order to be on the right side, so to speak, in the coming decade and live a life above the storm:

Guard my mind!

Each and every day I wake, my senses begin their work, and they at once begin to pick up on all things around me. When I lift my head in the morning, I hear the sound of my alarm, which is synced to the local radio station's morning show. From there, I shower and turn on my favorite podcast, listening on autopilot as I dress and prep my meals for the day. From there, I begin checking my emails, but hold on; before that, I must swipe through the handful of messages my phone carrier has sent me regarding some of the major world news for the day. And then I enter my car, and again, my senses are readily at work, taking all of the principles I am being fed from either my own musical selection or the selection of music that is being played on the local radio. But this influence on the soul, it doesn't stop there, for it appears every car I pass carries a bumper sticker or two—each plastered with principles from both Michael's Commander or Mr. Prince's master. I mustn't forget the billboards I pass each day on the freeway on my way to my office, for those, too, present a constant battle between both kingdoms. Then at the office, I cannot omit the office gossip between coworkers and every interaction between my colleagues and our customers. Opinions, facts, half-truths, all of them are constantly being disseminated and taken in by the senses.

But yet, the battle for my soul marches on, for I haven't yet checked the various social mediums that I currently subscribe to, and when I do, I immediately receive opposing principles from my network of thousands of followers. Thousands of people are disseminating principles that my senses have no choice but to absorb. Depending on how often I check them or how accustomed I have gotten to relying on them, this number could be multiplied 10-, 15-, or 20-fold. Repetition, repetition, repetition—my soul is slowly being transformed by whatever I continue absorbing on such platforms.

Let's now finish off the day.

After work, I head away from the office and off to the gym, where the senses of my eyes now kick into high gear, taking in all that is around me as I complete my early evening workout. If you've been to the gym at least once in the last decade—you get the idea. Upon leaving this mental and visual harrying, I receive numerous phone calls from family and friends, plus hundreds of messages on the several group chats that I have found myself a member of. Each one feeds my sensual appetite; each message represents either the side of good or the side of evil. As I settle in for the evening, the assault continues as I fall asleep to the sound of the television or the evening news, which aggressively bombards me again and again, battling fervently for undisputed control of my soul.

By the time I have again laid my head down to sleep for the night, I have undoubtedly been exposed to some millions of principles that are fighting for my allegiance.

A Better Way: "Civil Disobedience" Meets "Practicing the Presence"

Now that I have decided which government I will follow, I must follow, I have been left with the task of designing a better way. I must blaze a more formidable path to "guarding my mind" and protecting myself from the damning principles being disseminated by Mr. Prince and his master, thereby securing my future in spite of the circumstances and situations I find myself engulfed in due to the wily tricks of the side of darkness in the coming years. This idea of both civil disobedience and practicing the presence combined, I feel, presents me and all others a promising strategy that can at once be deployed for immediate action.

Those who champion this idea of civil disobedience have said that the external government, which the people have chosen to bring about their will, is equally liable to be abused and perverted before the people can effectively act through it. They have also said that, for practicality's sake, having no external government is also not a viable option in the immediate. What is an option, however, is ***better*** external government. As Thoreau wrote in ***Civil Disobedience***, "Every man should make known what kind of government would command his respect, and that will be one step toward obtaining it."

Well, in this case, now that I understand the fact, yes, the ***fact***, that external government is merely a reflection of either a healthy or poverty-stricken internal state, I must, first and foremost, make known the kind of internal government that fits my liking and begin at once adhering to it. Contrary to external government, however, I now know that I can, in fact, completely reject either internal government, the side of light, or the side of darkness. I can reject the one of ill and mischievous principles in favor of the one whose principles I most pressingly seek to align with. For as Thoreau noted, "All men recognize the right to revolution; that is, the right to refuse allegiance to, and to resist, the government, when its tyranny or its inefficiency are great and unendurable."

Is the government of Asbeel and his master tyrannical and inefficient? In his own words, "It is a wonderful thing when I see a man finally begin to unconsciously act out things like murder, lust, and adultery, and not even be aware of it, or be convicted by it. That is when I, my master, and his forces, have won." Or perhaps it is even more prevalent in his statement, "Our kingdom can be found wherever, and through whomever—even those that choose not to acknowledge us! You have perhaps seen our kingdom in many places and in many forms, and it is evidenced by things like hatred, discord, jealousy, fits of rage, selfish ambition, dissensions, factions, envy, drunkenness, orgies, and sexual immorality." These characteristics create an environment that is both tyrannical and inefficient in nature, formidable obstacles for creating and shaping a better world. Therefore, I must, in good conscience, refuse my allegiance to it in favor of its Adversary.

Now that I have made my ultimate, final decision and have pledged to refute any allegiance to the kingdom of darkness that Asbeel, or Mr. Prince, represents, I must decide in practical terms the nature in which I will seek to pursue his Adversary and His government, the kingdom of light. I must admit, in my most recent analysis of the situation based on an assessment of both my current life and how I have found myself at times a victim to both moral and immoral principles, the solution I have devised does not veer far from the path I found myself on prior to my encounter. This is what I had and have continued to term "practicing the presence," or the constant pursuit of the Father.

The book by the 17th-century brother I had mentioned earlier is called ***The Practice of the Presence of God.*** The basic theme of the message is the development of the awareness of the presence of the Father in one's life is, once mastered, the key by which all men must live and continue to live if he is to give his full allegiance to the government of Heaven. A man must strive to develop a keen sense of the Father in all his dealings, and he must take that sense, once he has mastered its development and attained it, with him wherever he finds himself. One must strive to keep his gaze entirely fixed on Him in faith—calmly, humbly, and lovingly, without allowing the appearance of anxious thoughts or emotions.

When one awakes in the morning, his mind must be fixed on Him. As he prepares for the day, his mind must be fastened on Him. In the midst of the chaotic traffic of the day, his mind must remain faithfully secured on Him and His presence. At the water cooler with colleagues and as he rummages through his lunch, his mind must be set and decided on Him. As he finishes out the day and heads to the gym for his evening workout, a sense of the Divine must still permeate his being. Then, even in the midst of his own home when his guards are lowered and he enjoys his evening dinner followed by a few moments of exposure to various mediums, he must remain 100 percent cognizant of the presence of the Father.

Many who read this will likely dismiss this as some utopian dream that cannot be realized amidst the busy world that we live, and so I will take the time to challenge this assumption. In order to do so, I must first remind you of what one's focus should be and where it should be placed. When one is focused on the "Divine," as it has been coined, he is really focusing on the One who rules over the government to which he has given his allegiance. In other words, the gaze and focus of his mind can always be found on the King who rules over the government of Heaven, of which he is a citizen. Because the King is the embodiment of the kingdom, then thoughts of the "Divine," or the King, are really thoughts directed toward the kingdom in which a person finds himself living. So, in essence, one's thoughts of the Divine, or the King, are really thoughts of the government of which he is a citizen.

Does this sound familiar? In our earthly country, it has been said that a citizen should always strive to be a law-abiding citizen. If one is to be a law-abiding citizen, he must at all times be aware, if not subconsciously, that he is a citizen representing the government of the country in which he lives. So, when he awakes in the morning, he must remember his citizenship. When he prepares for his day, he must remember this citizenship. When he finds himself at the water cooler and at lunch, rummaging away at the previous night's leftovers, he must remain cognizant of the fact that he must remain a law-abiding citizen. From his work to the gym, and from the gym to his home, and from his home to the dinner table and to the couch, he is always "practicing the presence," or reminding himself that he is a servant of his country and must remain in right standing.

The key is that the government of Heaven is no different, except for the fact that the King Himself is the embodiment of the country and any thoughts of the King are actually thoughts of His government or His kingdom. So, in essence, when one can train himself to be aware of this presence at all times, aware of the fact that he is a servant of the government, he will align himself totally to that government and be able to effectively "guard his mind" against all of the wily tricks of the adversary. ***You are what you are continually hearing; you are what you are continually seeing.*** There is nothing on Earth as powerful as the human will because the very nature of will implies self-control. The will of man controls the destiny of man. The seat of the will is the conscious and the subconscious mind. A man is whatever is in his subconscious mind, and whoever controls the subconscious mind controls the man. ***Whoever controls the heart controls the life. If you want to control the man, you must control the heart, and the heart is controlled through constant repetition. The more a thing is repeated, the more the subconscious mind is impacted. It all comes down to a battle for the soul. The soul is a collection of the mind, the will, and the emotions. The battle in life is for the soul of man.***

It is with our minds that we become slaves to our masters. The mind is the battleground, and it is the place where the greatest conflict is. More trouble is in the mind of man than in the wallet of man. It is due to this conflict that people go to bed tired and wake up tired. It is due to this conflict that many people get sleep, but they never get rest. It is due to this conflict that people find that their minds are in turmoil all night long, and they wrestle in their sleep, caught up in warfare. The enemy is after the mind because the mind is the battleground. Worry, stress, nervous breakdowns, feelings of quitting, and feelings of failure. The desire to quit on one's dream. The desire to never get up and resort to giving up on their dream. The fight, the real fight, is in the mind.

This, I must conclude, is the key to an effective life, an effective decade, and the foundation of any fulfillment on the way toward completion of one's destiny.

As I sit here, I find myself once again thinking deeply of the following possibility: Suppose I could think any thought or dream any dream that my heart desired. Suppose I could use this ability to see into the future 5, 10, or perhaps even 50 years down the road. Suppose I could ask any question and get any answer regarding the future and the destiny of the world. A secret, perhaps, to help those currently living and those who will one day inhabit Planet Earth live a life free from the oppression and the hopelessness that has come to torture and torment so many in our days. I have supposed before, and I now suppose again, but this time, I am not without answer:

Indeed, the focus of one's mind, body, spirit, and soul must be in alignment with the government of Heaven, one must find himself in a state of complete disobedience to the adversary, and he must each and every day strive to master the practice of the Father's presence. ***For light is to darkness what love is to fear; in the presence of one, the other disappears.*** A true formula for conquering ***the fear within.***

At this moment, as I think back to the trickster's little riddle, I fold my arms, lean back in my chair, and smile.

CPSIA information can be obtained
at www.ICGtesting.com
Printed in the USA
LVHW052125201021
701012LV00001B/4/J

9 781641 466806